Healthy Bodies Also Die
A Claire Burke Mystery
(Book 7)

by
Emma Pivato

For information, email Cozy Cat Press, cozycatpress@gmail.com or visit our website at: www.cozycatpress.com

COZY CAT
PRESS

ISBN: 978-1-946063-96-0
Printed in the United States of America

10 9 8 7 6 5 4 3 2 1

Dedication:

This book is dedicated to my daughter, Juliana Pivato, and my son-in-law, Marc Couroux, who have strongly encouraged my literary efforts from the very beginning

Acknowledgements:

As always, I thank my husband, Joe Pivato, for his steady support.

Thank you to the Super 8 Motel staff in Leduc who make me so welcome when I go there to write.

And finally, thank you to Aziza Pivato, my 13-year-old granddaughter, who carefully edited this book and discovered various errors along the way!

Table of Contents

Chapter 1: Lifestyle Change

Claire had decided. She was going on a diet. She had read about it, thought about it, planned for it—and now the time had come. She was ready to take the first step—to step on the scale. Shoeless and in light pajamas, Claire placed one foot on the scale and then, after an additional moment to tighten her resolve, the other. She closed her eyes and steadied herself, taking a deep breath and letting it all out. Finally she looked down.

Shock! The 20 pounds she had talked for a long time about needing to lose had mysteriously morphed into 28! How had that happened? Claire thought back over the past 15 years since her daughter, Jessica, had been born. She recalled her occasional lunches with friends. *They are so rare they could hardly account for this gain,* she argued to herself.

But how greedily she had approached those scattered moments of talking and laughing together. How she had justified filling up her plate with every food item that intrigued her. She remembered with shame, shoveling large forks full into her mouth like a squirrel storing up nuts for the winter. *To fill up the emptiness,* she thought sadly. *To make up for all those times alone with Jessie, unable to go out with her or to have people over because of her bad spells, her unpredictable seizures and sudden screaming attacks. Other people don't have to live like that. All I had was food!*

Even as she said it, however, she knew it was a lie, the self-pity speaking. Her husband, Dan, wasn't overweight, after all—and he had lived the same life as her. Claire had been slowly facing up to this weakness in herself over the past year, her third year of running the Co-op where her three friends/clients lived. She had even talked about her weight problem with one of them, Roscoe, a man now in his mid-thirties with Down syndrome. He had the same problem and Claire suspected that it was because he was trying to fill up the same emptiness.

Roscoe had spent many years in an institution before his parents had decided to move from Calgary to Edmonton and to bring him with them. He had become the third resident in a home that Claire had established with the help of friends and family, especially her close friend, Tia. Tia's sister-in-law, Mavis, who lived with multiple disabilities that left her fully dependent on others and confined to a wheelchair, was also in the home. The third client was Bill, Mavis' wannabe beau. Because of his autism, he tended to become overly focused on certain issues to the virtual exclusion of everything else and this made it impossible for him to live without support and direction. One of his major obsessions was Mavis, whom he referred to in his characteristic, singsong voice as Mae-Mae.

These had been better years for Claire, engaging her mind on a daily basis to grapple with her clients' respective programs and to create the best life she could for them. And she and Dan had more help at home with Jessie now so they weren't as homebound as they used to be. But the habits of all those hard, early years had made them reclusive, not quick to take advantage of social opportunities or to plan ahead for attending social events. Claire craved these more than Dan and hence she ate—and drank more wine than necessary at times— –to compensate.

Two months previously, Claire had joined a gym, Women's World, thinking that would be the answer to both toning up and trimming down. But in the weeks that followed, she had attended only sporadically, riding a bike for 10 minutes, using a few machines more or less correctly and then settling on the exercise table where she did some pelvic lifts and air bicycling and then some minor crunching that mostly involved resting.

Finally. Claire had accepted that this was not enough and inquired about the availability of a personal trainer to help her get an effective program going. She had met with Caroline, a young woman with a perfect face and figure who could easily have been a model, and they had begun working together. But Caroline was much in demand and the only time she could meet with her regularly was at 6 a.m. Tuesday mornings. That was today.

Claire quickly collected everything she would need for her day at the Co-op and jumped in her car. Ten minutes later, she was at the gym and paused at the doorstep to take a few deep breaths of the early summer morning air. *Maybe these six o'clock sessions won't be so bad after all,* she thought to herself.

Caroline had, as usual, left the door open for her since no one was at the front desk yet and no other clients were there that early in the morning. Claire carefully locked it behind her, as she had been instructed, and quickly changed into her gym shoes. She pushed through the gate and walked back to the exercise table where the two always met, rounded the divider that separated it from the rest of the gym and spotted Caroline immediately. She was lying flat on her back on the table, but a heavy barbell lay across her neck!

Caroline's eyes were bulging and her tongue was sticking out and Claire knew in an instant there was no life there. She stood stunned, trying to decide what to do next. But her body was not waiting for direction. She rushed to a nearby garbage receptacle, tore off the lid and threw up her breakfast. Even as she did so, she noted that it was empty except for a pair of disposable rubber gloves at the bottom.

Claire then grabbed for her phone. Ten minutes later, she heard the siren and shortly after, two beat cops came bustling in. But moments later, the door opened a second time to admit Inspector McCoy. "How...?" Claire asked weakly, still shaking from her recent discovery.

"I have you flagged," he replied. "Whenever *you* are involved, they call me.

For a few seconds, Claire felt a flush of pleasure. But then McCoy added, "*I* know how to handle you when you start interfering with an investigation."

After a cursory look at the body, the cause of death being obvious, McCoy's nose led him to the garbage can. He saw the gloves coated in vomit and glared at Claire. "I couldn't help it," she said miserably. He took her statement then and she was free to go, just in time for her 8 o'clock shift at the co-op.

Claire greeted Roscoe, the only one of The Three Musketeers, as they were affectionately known, who was still at home. Then she looked longingly across the street at Tia's house, but Tia was away working at the hospital where she now managed the entire maintenance department.

"Wha *wong,* Claih?" Roscoe asked anxiously. He was always very sensitive to her moods.

Claire looked at him. She did not want to upset him. He had been involved in enough murder and violence the last few years, some of it directed at him. "Something happened at the gym, Roscoe."

"Wha *hoppen?*"

"My trainer died," she said weakly. "I don't want to talk about it right now ...okay, Roscoe?" He just looked at her as if he knew there was more to the story than that, but said nothing.

The plan that day had been for Claire and Roscoe to visit an art center designed for persons with cognitive limitations, but Claire did not feel up to it. Mostly she felt like crawling into bed with a good escapist novel but that was not possible.

"Let's make cookies, Roscoe!" *To hell with the diet!* she thought angrily.

They had just put the last pan in the oven when the doorbell rang. Roscoe opened the door.

"It for you, Claih." he called out. "Da policemom!"

Because of the way Roscoe said this, Claire knew immediately that it was Inspector McCoy. His previous interactions with Roscoe had not endeared him to the young man. Claire invited McCoy into the kitchen and placed a cup of coffee in front of him along with a plate of freshly baked gingersnaps that she knew he favored. *Might as well butter him up!* she said to herself sourly.

After consuming half his coffee and a couple of cookies, McCoy turned to her and pulled out his mini-computer to record her responses. "Go over it again," he requested. "Why were you there so early and tell me everything you noticed from the time you parked your car."

"I've been going to that gym off and on for the past two months but this was only my third visit with a trainer—her."

"What did you need a trainer for?" he asked suspiciously. "Frankly, you don't look to me like the type who generally frequents trainers!"

"Yeah, that's exactly why!" she said wryly. Claire was sitting across from him at the table but he had stood up to ask this question, a classic interview technique for intimidating clients. Claire didn't look intimidated, however; what he saw instead was the hurt look in her eyes.

Something happened then which neither of them was able to explain later. Inspector McCoy—cool, cocky, arrogant Donald McCoy—leaned over and gently kissed Claire full on the lips. Claire was initially startled and horrified but then found herself, for no identifiable reason, kissing him back.

Neither of them noticed the shadow coming around the door to the kitchen and then withdrawing abruptly. A moment later, Claire pulled away, placed her hand over her mouth and just looked at him. He could not interpret her expression and, in fact, she could not have interpreted it herself.

"I'm sorry!" he said, hoarsely. "I shouldn't have done that! Please, let's just forget it ever happened."

"I'm sorry, too," she said. "I could have stopped you sooner. But I'm glad if it means you can at least see me as more than 'an interfering busybody'."

McCoy winced when he heard her words, recalling the time she'd overheard him describing her as exactly that to a colleague. "You are!" he said finally, "but you've done some good work—work that I wouldn't have been able to do in some cases ... and you and Tia have also put yourself at serious risk at times."

"I know", she said softly. "And I also know that you have put *yourself* at risk on a couple of occasions to protect us." Claire was thinking especially of a recent event where he had moved quickly to retrieve her and Aunt Gus from some motorcycle hoods. "Why did you do that? You're supposed to wait for back-up in situations like that."

"You *know* why!" he said softly.

Claire nodded her head, acknowledging the strange attraction that existed between them.

Roscoe was still listening behind the door. He could not help himself. Later he would ask Claire about what he had seen and heard.

"Back to business," McCoy said abruptly. "This time I really need your help—but that doesn't mean you should take it upon yourself to solve this puzzle single-handed and put yourself in harm's way like you usually do!"

"How can I help?" Claire asked simply. She was still feeling disoriented from all that had happened that day, including this most recent event, and couldn't think fast enough to fire off one of her usual responses.

"This situation is unique." The gym is for women only and apparently the rule there is that any time a man is on the premises he has to be announced. This isn't going to work well for carrying out a proper investigation. We have, of course, processed the crime scene but the gym was kept closed for that purpose. Now we're out of there and don't have ongoing access. I need an insider's view on what's going on. I need someone who can encourage people to talk about it and who can pick up on any useful gossip."

"And that would be me, right?" Claire asked.

McCoy nodded. He stood up to leave. She stood up to accompany him to the door but he closed the gap between them and grabbed her hand. "Please be careful," he admonished. "Watch out for body language and tell me everything you learn as soon as you learn it. If at any time you feel negative vibes coming from someone you interview, I want to know about it immediately, so I can provide suitable monitoring and protection."

"What you mean is you want to cramp my style!" Claire replied with a faint tinge of jocularity.

"I just want you to be safe—so don't forget!" he said tersely. And with that he was out the door.

Claire poured herself another cup of coffee, sat down at the table and munched absent-mindedly on a cookie. *Why,* she asked herself.

"Why, Claih? Why you *do* dat?" She looked up and saw Roscoe standing there before her. He had often surprised her with his sudden presence. Despite his bulk and the low muscle tone associated with his condition, he had always had the capacity to creep into and out of a room like a shadow.

"What?" she replied, raising her eyebrows in a vain effort to recapture the client/supervisor relationship, but it didn't work.

"*You* know," he said. "Dan not like ..." He couldn't go on, but there was a worried look on his face.

"That is true," Claire said sadly. "I can't tell him right now. Maybe later."

Roscoe made a clumsy attempt at the universal 'zip my lips' sign and then asked again, "Buh why?"

"I don't know," Claire replied, looking ashamed and miserable. "I don't know why ... why he kissed me.... and why I kissed him back. Maybe I'm lonesome. Maybe I'm bored. Maybe I just had a really shocking, horrible experience and needed some closeness. I don't *know!*"

Roscoe looked confused. "Dan *good!* Me *like Dan!*"

Claire recognized the stubborn caste to his face and read it clearly. After three years of working with him, she well knew his strengths and limitations. He could not understand the reasons she had provided and he could only fall back on what he knew for certain: 'Dan good'. Claire felt more alone than ever. She felt very close to Roscoe but there would always be that gap between them that neither could bridge. The limitations in his very genes made it impossible.

Chapter 2: A Confusing Time

It was ten o'clock Saturday morning and Claire was relaxing in her favorite reclining chair in the living room with a second cup of coffee. She had no work or other compelling duties to perform and Jessie had gone to the Science Centre with her assistant to watch an Imax film and then have lunch.

Jessie could not see but somehow she seemed to enjoy these films anyway. Maybe it was the surround sound or the images cast in different lights emanating from the enormous screen. Her blindness was cortical so her retinas could still register light and shadows and the shifts between images, although the optic nerve behind them could not organize the images into something that could be meaningfully interpreted.

Claire suddenly felt restless and wondered what to do. She was not much good with idle relaxation. And constantly clanging away at the back of her mind was the 'stolen kiss' with Donald McCoy and Roscoe's horrified reaction. Whenever something this unsettling had happened to her in the past few years, something she could not share with Dan, she had always been able to tell Tia. But not this time! Much as they had gone through together and much as they thought alike on certain issues, they were very different in some ways. Tia took a black and white view on moral issues and could be quite judgmental while Claire blurred the boundaries more and was generally more charitable and forgiving to others who had crossed a line.

I guess I am more like Aunt Gus than I thought I was. Claire grinned to herself, thinking of her aunt's antics. *Maybe she would understand!* Claire picked up the phone.

"Hi, Aunt Gus. How *are* you?"

"Fine. We're leaving for Victoria on Friday. I was going to call you."

"Oh? Why are you going there? How long will you be gone?"

"We'll be there for three weeks visiting John's daughter. Anne just got a position with a big investment firm and she wants to discuss various issues with her father and to show off her new apartment to us. It was quite a coup getting one that large and that central in Victoria's housing market, apparently."

"Any chance we could get together today for a visit?" Claire asked.

"Sure! Why don't the four of us go out to supper together somewhere? Aunt Gus didn't like to cook and, despite the fact that her financial circumstances were considerably rosier than they had been before her recent marriage, she also didn't like to pay. Claire understood by the vague way Gus presented the invitation that this way they would split the bill at worst or Dan would offer to pay, as he often did, at best.

"No. I meant alone."

"Is something wrong?"

"No. Nothing big. Just something I want to run by you."

"Okay. Do you want to meet somewhere for lunch?"

"No. Could you come here? I have the house to myself. Dan's out of town and Jessie has gone out for the day with her assistant. I don't expect her back until after three."

"Hmmm. Not like you to turn down a lunch date, Claire. Must be something serious. I'll be there in an hour." Aunt Gus hung up the phone abruptly. She had never been good at small talk.

"So what's on your mind?" Aunt Gus asked when she walked in the door later.

"Uh. Let's have lunch first. I made an omelet. And after that I have some nice lemon bars I made yesterday to go with our coffee."

"No bars for me," Gustava said cheerfully. "Got to watch my figure. I'm married to a younger man, you know. Have to keep him interested!"

Claire rolled her eyes at this latest example of her 72-year-old aunt's incessant vanity but said nothing. After they ate, she brought out the coffee and two bars for herself on a plate and suggested that they sit in the family room. Once settled, Gus took a sip of her black coffee and then turned to Claire. "Okay, what's up?" she asked.

Claire told her everything that had happened with the recent murder and the inspector's subsequent behavior and then waited anxiously for her aunt's response. But Gus said nothing. Well?" Claire finally asked.

"Well, what?" Gus retorted. "What's the big deal? Look what happened to me?" And Gus was off on a rehash of her still recent romance of two years ago with the man who was now her husband.

Claire listened patiently, all the time wondering why she had not shared this information with Tia instead. Tia, at least, really cared about her. It was hard for Gus, given her narcissism, to care about anybody but herself. Although in recent years she had seemed to develop some genuine interest in Jessie. Claire thought it was because Jessie demanded little of her psychologically, certainly not the rendering of a carefully thought out opinion on such a delicate subject as the one Claire had just shared. And, of course, her aunt's relationship with

John seemed quite genuine and it really had been a touching story, accidentally rediscovering each other after all those years. *But is it still more of a romantic fairytale in Gus' mind than a real thing?* Claire wondered.

The visit continued with Claire making perfunctory responses to her aunt's ongoing tales about her new and exciting life. But finally Gus noticed that Claire was not her usual self. "You're not still fretting over that little incident, are you?" she asked.

"No, you're probably right," Claire responded. "I'm probably making too much out of it. It was just one of those fluky things that happen sometimes." But that was not what she was thinking. She had obviously made a mistake in sharing this information with Gus. Not only had her aunt given her no useful advice. Now Claire was concerned that she might not keep the information to herself. "Let's just forget about it, like you suggested," she said, turning to her aunt. And please don't share this with anyone. It's very embarrassing."

Gus nodded in agreement and the visit soon ended.

Chapter 3: Fitness Penance

Just before Claire dropped off to sleep that night, she realized that Dan would be home from his business trip in two more days. Before that, she thought, some serious thinking and restitution would have to be done.

The next day was Sunday and Claire sat alone at the breakfast table with Jessie. Her assistant would arrive at noon and stay until eight. After Claire finished feeding Jessie and herself breakfast, she placed Jessie in her hammock to swing gently back and forth for a while and 'digest her food'. Claire used this excuse quite frequently when she was alone with her and needed some downtime herself.

As she sat in a rocking chair near Jessie, moving back and forth in harmony with Jessie's swaying, she thought about Friday's events. Donald McCoy actually wanted her help this time to figure out who had killed Caroline. *That* was a first!

But that moment that had happened between them. What was that all about? Who was he in his private life? What had happened to him in the past?

She didn't know the answers to any of these questions and had no clear way of acquiring them. All she could do was look at herself and her own behavior. Why had she felt that sudden surge of attraction? *Classic case of purple prose*, she thought sourly: swash-buckling hero saves damsel in distress! That charged moment between her and McCoy had been nothing more than a sudden, dramatic release from the dull routine and tedium of daily life.

But I like my life for the most part! she told herself. *And I love my husband and daughter. Also, I have good friends whom I care about very much, including Aunt Gus, odd as she is. There is just not enough fun in it— too much 'same old; same old'. Dan is great but he's not much for fun and adventure. I miss that. Solving these mysteries in the past few years has been the most exciting thing I can remember ever happening to me! But it's the mysteries that have been exciting, not Inspector Don McCoy. I don't even like him very much. So why? Why did that happen? Why didn't I stop him? Because it took me by surprise? Because I was curious? Because I wanted to see where it would go?*

When she reached that point in her reasoning, Claire just shook her head. Of course, she didn't want to see where it would go! But this man had been treating her like a useless pest for a long time. Admittedly, he had been softening up in some of their recent cases. But a kiss? Why? That's all she really wanted to know. That and to know that from now on he would treat her differently—with more respect, more like an equal and not just like some bored, nosy housewife.

What can I do? she asked herself. *What can I do to keep this new, closer relationship with him but not let it become personal?* But she knew the answer. She was going to have to start exercising seriously, demonstrate to the people at the gym a real change of heart so they wouldn't be suspicious when she was hanging around more. And demonstrate to him that she was seriously looking for the murderer!

The next morning, Monday, Claire had the day off because of working a double shift at the co-op the Thursday before so once Jessie left for school, Claire headed for the gym. Claire explained to the person at the front desk that she needed a new trainer and was soon introduced to a tall, rather grim-looking woman who did not seem particularly happy to be there. However she *did* seem happy to be assigned a new client to train because that was where the money was.

Claire arranged to meet with Candace Turnblatt at 6:30 on Tuesday and Thursday mornings. That would allow her to still be at the co-op by 8 when her shift started. Dan had no trips scheduled for the next few months so he'd be able to get Jessie out the door those mornings. And if something came up so he couldn't, then she would just re-schedule.

The next morning was her very first session with this person and Claire arrived with mixed emotions. This Candace would not be as good as Caroline, of course. Caroline had told her she was the best, that she knew the most of all the trainers there about exercising. But Claire was in for a pleasant surprise. Candace didn't say much, but when she spoke every word counted.

After collecting some history, Candace handed Claire two 8-kilogram kettle bells and instructed her to walk around the gym twice with one in each hand. Claire glanced over at her at various points in her two treks around the room and was surprised to see that Candace's eyes had remained constantly upon her. Caroline had taken opportunities like that to check her email or to furtively fit in a couple of lunges when the supervisor was not around, just to keep her own fitness level up.

On her return, Candace had some words for Claire. "We need to work on your posture and balance. It looks to me like your biceps are very strong; you told me that you regularly lift your 90-pound daughter. But your triceps are weaker, causing extra stress on your shoulder muscles as you compensate. And by the way you picked up your right hand kettle bell, I would guess that the bicep in your right arm has been injured. Just move that arm across your body like this and tell me if you feel anything."

Claire did as requested and winced. "Oh!" she exclaimed. "That hurt!"

"Yes. You've been working around some injury there for a while, haven't you?"

"I guess so. I never really take time to notice. Life is so complicated; I just carry on."

Candace said nothing more but put Claire through a series of arm exercises then, instructing her not to go beyond the point where it hurt. She then had her walk up and down the stairs a couple of times, watching her closely as she went.

After the arm exercises, she informed Claire that it looked like her left arm had been compensating for the weaker right arm for a long time and had been overstrained as a result. After the stair walking, she told Claire that she walked with her head forward and her shoulders hunched. "What position do you like to sit in at home?" she asked.

Claire gave a guilty smile. "I enjoy my recliner where I can put my feet up and rest my neck on the back of the chair."

"Yes, that makes sense. The way you walk I would say you have shortened hamstrings and also you're taking more of your weight on your right leg for some reason. Do you have any health care coverage for physio?"

Claire nodded her head mutely.

Candace scribbled down a name and number on a piece of paper and handed it to her. "This guy is really good and he's quite close to you. I'd like you to see him as soon as possible for a better assessment than I can do. I want to know what exercises are safe for you to do and what are not before we get into anything more serious than some mild cardio."

Claire nodded her head in agreement, feeling somewhat stunned by all this new information. "Caroline never said anything about all this!" she said with a questioning note in her voice.

"Can't help that," Candace said tersely. "That's all for today. I'll see you on Thursday morning." Without saying anything further, she turned around and headed for the private back area of the gym.

Claire just stood there, trying to take in all that she'd been told. At that moment, Gladys, the supervisor, walked by and asked her how she liked her new trainer.

"She's different from Caroline," Claire responded. "All business!"

"Yeah. I overheard some of what she was telling you. We should have started you with her."

Chapter 4: A Change of Heart, A Change of Focus

The next week Claire met with the physical therapist Candace had recommended. Jackson Dawes was relatively young, in his early thirties Claire thought. But he really seemed to have a deep understanding of how the human body worked. After taking her through a series of arm movements and also having her walk back and forth so he could check out her posture, Jackson sent Claire off to get some x-rays.

Two days later, Claire returned for a follow-up visit. "The results indicate the presence of a mild scoliosis and some calcification in your right shoulder which has likely been there for some time, probably the result of an old injury," Jackson informed her as he studied the x-ray report he'd received. Do you remember when it happened?"

"No," Claire replied. "I know I've had pain in it for a long time but I've just been working around it."

"Well, your body accommodates to these kinds of injuries but there's always a price to pay. In your case, that price is reduced range of motion in your shoulder."

"What should I do about it and what should I tell my trainer?" Claire asked.

"I'm going to give you some exercises to do and if you do them regularly and see me for some therapy sessions for a few weeks I think you should be able to get back most of your range. I'm also going to write a note for your trainer advising her as to what I think she should be working on. The important thing for you to remember is do not work past the point of pain."

Claire went home from her first session with Jackson feeling shocked and angry. She was angry at herself for neglecting her body and angry at her life for being so complicated and difficult that she could have undergone this level of injury without even noticing. Claire vowed to herself that this was going to stop now. She would search for the killer at the gym and she would continue her efforts to lose weight. But her primary motivation was no longer to look good or to save the world by unearthing one killer at a time. It was to get fit and to undo as much of the damage to her body as she could.

When she next met with Candace, there was a distinct change in Claire's attitude. She no longer made self-deprecating jokes about her condition and lack of motivation and she tried harder to complete the tasks that Candace set for her without complaining. Furthermore, she started to go to the gym on her own between her workout sessions with Candace. Gradually, during their sessions together, she had learned how to use various pieces of equipment correctly so she would not hurt herself any further, and how to avoid any exercise that would exacerbate the injury in her shoulder.

Over the next two weeks, Claire began to notice that she was feeling better, more energetic and less short of breath when she exerted herself. During her regular sessions at the gym she began to recognize some of the other regular attendees and struck up conversations with a few of them. She also spent her time on the bike or the elliptical or the rower looking around and listening to snatches of conversations from others. One day she overheard two of the regular trainers discussing Caroline in hushed tones.

A tall, rangy redhead, who carried out many of the group 'boot camp' sessions at the back of the gym, was talking to a younger, much shorter woman—blond, pink-faced and overweight. "Who could have gotten in here that early in the morning, Ellie?" the younger woman asked.

"It could have been anybody, Marjorie," Ellie replied. "Caroline was expecting an early morning client and she often left the door unlocked on those occasions. She wasn't supposed to, but Caroline was not one for following the rules."

"Or it could have been somebody with a key who knew the security code, another staff member!" Marjorie retorted, and gave a visible shiver. "Or maybe the client did it! It wouldn't be a stretch given the way Caroline treated everyone!" Marjorie offered with a note of spite in her voice.

Claire winced when she heard this since she was that mysterious client but just then another patron approached her to ask if she was going to be through with the rower soon and she lost the remaining remarks of the conversation. However, as her gym days passed she heard more and more bits of conversation referencing Caroline from various trainers and clients. Many of these alluded to Caroline's general unpopularity but a couple also involved speculations about a former relationship that had gone sour.

Finally, Claire overheard something that could provide a possible lead. Ellie was discussing the matter with another trainer one day and Claire heard her say, "You knew her better than anybody here. What do *you* think? The other trainer murmured a response but it was too soft for Claire to hear. *I have to talk to this woman,* Claire thought, but she didn't even know her name.

Two days later, Claire returned to the gym. After changing into her gym shoes, she walked slowly towards the back, keeping her eyes open. The trainer she wanted to talk to was there, in the part of the gym near the table. Claire was ready to make her move! She walked quickly over to the table that fortunately was not in use and hopped up on it. Then she started doing various exercises including one that involved some arm work. She threw her arms back over her head as she lay flat on her back and then raised her body, stretching her arms far forward while holding her knees at right angles to her body and her lower legs in a table top position. Claire proceeded gently at first, biding her time, but once the woman was close enough to her so she would logically be the first responder, Claire reached forward vigorously and then clutched her arm while emitting a sharp scream!

Predictably, the woman came running. All staff members were primed to watch out for potential liability issues. "What happened?" she inquired urgently.

"I have a right shoulder problem and I think I strained it!" Claire moaned, clutching her arm.

"Let me help you down from there," the woman said, supporting Claire's good arm. Claire stumbled down from the table still clutching her arm and endeavoring to look faint and in pain.

"I'll get you a drink of water. We have some water bottles in our staff fridge," the woman offered.

"What I really need is a nice, strong Starbucks coffee—and someone to keep me company while I drink it," Claire declaimed, rubbing her arm gingerly.

The woman looked hesitant and Claire noted the supervisor standing nearby. "I was going to rebook with my trainer. I only have two lessons left—but now I don't know. Maybe this wasn't such a good idea after all!" Claire muttered, moaning slightly.

The supervisor stepped forward at that point and directed her attention to the trainer. "Why don't you take Claire over to Starbucks, Sylvia? Coffee is on us for both of you!" She turned to Claire and said, "You just rest a while and I'm sure your arm will feel better. And if you do decide to renew your training sessions, I'll see to it that you get a couple of training sessions free if you choose the package of 24."

"Let's go!" Sylvia said, taking hold of Claire's good arm gently. "A couple of lattes sound good right now!" and she looked at Gladys, the supervisor, meaningfully.

"Get whatever you want," Gladys added hastily. "And don't feel you have to hurry back," she added, turning to Sylvia.

At the Starbucks, Claire ordered her favorite drink, a large 'Flat White" but she asked for de-caf. Caffeine didn't seem to be agreeing with her lately. Sylvia settled on a caramel macchiato and sipped away on it with great pleasure. "How's your arm feeling now?" she asked.

Claire suddenly remembered the need to look pained and she replied in a dull voice, "It's not hurting as much but I still think this gym thing may be a bad idea for me. I should just leave it to you jocks!"

Sylvia looked insulted. "I don't consider myself a jock," she replied. "I just want to be healthy and live a long, healthy life. That seems to be a reasonable goal to me!" And as she said this, she gave Claire a long, faintly censorious look.

"Oh!" Claire said, looking a bit flustered. "I didn't really mean that! I guess I'm just upset about what happened, seeing Caroline like that when I walked in that morning. I just kept thinking that it doesn't matter how healthy and perfect you are. You're still mortal and can die or be destroyed at any time. It has kind of made me re-evaluate whether or not I want to waste the time and energy required for all that exercising."

"It must have been a terrible shock!" Sylvia agreed, speaking more softly now. "But it's not as if it happens every day. In fact it's never happened here. In the three years I've been a trainer at this gym the worst thing I've ever seen happen is a strained wrist!"

"Well, it *did* happen!" Claire said stubbornly. "And every time I get on that exercise table I can't help reliving it. I think that's why I hurt myself this morning. I wasn't concentrating on what I was doing because I was remembering."

"Well, maybe you should just stay off the table, then," Sylvia suggested.

"*That* won't change anything!" Claire retorted. "The fact is that there's a murderer around there somewhere and the most likely possibility is that it's one of you trainers … maybe *my* new trainer for all I know. She's a kind of cold, funny person!'

"Oh, I doubt that!" Sylvia said, and clamped her mouth shut.

Claire saw her opening and took a couple of seconds to quietly congratulate herself for how clever she was! "Why not?" she said. "Do you have a better suspect in mind? Everybody else seems a lot more normal than *her!*"

Sylvia paused for a moment and then said rather tersely, "Caroline had an ex and he wasn't a very nice guy. They went together quite a while and he overnighted at her house a lot. He could have got hold of her gym key and copied it. He could have used that to get in that morning."

"Wow!" Claire replied. "Did you tell that to the police?"

"No, I didn't want to get involved. I have to work here."

Claire failed to see the logic of that particular line of reasoning but succeeded in not saying so—for which she again congratulated herself. "Tell *me* and I'll pass it on. And I won't say where I heard about him if you don't want me to."

Sylvia looked at her doubtfully.

"It's either that or I'm out of here. Good thing I haven't renewed my training sessions yet. I realize now that I just can't deal with this level of uncertainty!"

After a pause, Sylvia said, *"Fine,* but I don't want *anyone* to know where you heard it. If you promise me that I'll tell you." Claire nodded her head soberly.

"Not everybody liked Caroline," Sylvia went on, speaking in a slow, reflective manner. "But *I* did. I admired her hutzpah! She was beautiful and in peak condition—and she knew it. But that doesn't mean she was arrogant exactly, like some people thought. I'd say she was more naïve and self-centered. She didn't even notice when she was stepping on other people's toes and that's no way to make friends! But she had a good side, too. She loved animals, particularly cats. She had a big, beautiful cat, Fergus, and now I'm stuck with him because there was nobody else to take him."

Claire thought quickly. "I might know a good place he could go," she said. "But first I'd have to know more about Caroline and how she treated him and what he's like."

Sylvia's eyes lit up at that but just as she opened her mouth to respond her phone rang. "Oh, oh. Probably my client came early. I'll have to leave," she said. But when she answered the phone she was told that her next client had cancelled.

"Then let's get some more coffee and maybe a treat," Claire suggested. She'd been eying some cinnamon rolls that looked quite tasty. *"I'll* pay this time. I want to hear more about this Fergus character!"

For the next half hour, Sylvia chatted about Caroline and Fergus, and about Caroline's relationship and how she'd actually been quite a lonely person despite all her obvious physical advantages. Claire carefully steered the conversation towards possible enemies and acquired the contact information for the ex-boyfriend. She also discovered that Caroline's parents had both died in a car accident when Caroline was 15. That was only six months after the family had moved from Calgary to Edmonton and she'd been placed in a foster home.

"*That* might explain whatever personality issues she had that caused people to dislike her," Claire responded sagely, recalling a previous psychology course she'd taken.

"Ya *think?*" was Sylvia's laconic reply, leaving Claire feeling a bit foolish.

"Did Caroline have any other close relatives?" she asked.

Sylvia just looked at her and Claire suddenly realized why. "Oh, of *course,* not!" she exclaimed, answering her own question. "Otherwise she'd have had a place to go. But what will happen to her estate then?"

"I have *no* idea!" Sylvia responded coolly. She shifted in her chair and it looked to Claire like she was about to get up and leave. Sylvia was obviously not comfortable sharing personal information about someone she'd considered a friend. But Claire persisted, wanting to find out more. "There must have been *someone* she was close to, apart from you. You said that you only met her three years ago when you started working here!"

"Not that I know of," Sylvia said vaguely.

"Maybe the police will find some correspondence on her computer so they can track her contacts down," Claire offered, but Sylvia said nothing. "What about her last foster family?" Claire continued. "Did she stay in touch with them?"

"I don't think so. She didn't have much positive to say about them." Sylvia hesitated for a moment. It was clear to Claire that she had something else and was debating whether or not to share it. Claire waited patiently, endeavoring to look as sympathetic as possible. *I wish that Tia was here,* she thought to herself. *She's always better in these situations than I am.*

Sylvia started putting on her coat. It was obvious that she'd had just about enough. "I *know* you've thought of something else! *Please* tell me!" Claire entreated. "I just need to know there's some lead to follow up outside the gym or I can't keep coming. It's too frightening, thinking all the time that it must be one of you!"

"No, I can't do that!" Sylvia replied firmly. "I promised Caroline."

"Okay, I understand," Claire said with a note of resignation in her voice. "I will just go back now and let Gladys know that we've talked things over but I really have decided that I can't continue. I'm going to ask her for a refund for the two sessions I have left, given the circumstances." Claire stood up with a decisive look on her face.

"No, wait!" Sylvia said. "There *is* something else and it might help!" Claire sat down and raised her eyebrows but said nothing.

"There *were* some relatives—her mother's brother, Frank, and his wife, Ivy, and their daughter, Vanessa. They live in Calgary."

"Then why didn't *they* take Caroline in when her parents died?"

"The wife was against it, apparently. She thought Caroline would have been a bad influence on their daughter who was two years younger than her. At least, that's what Caroline told me."

"Why would she think that?"

"Well, there it gets complicated and I really, *really* don't want to get into it right now. Anyway, I must get back to the gym now. My next client will be arriving in five minutes!"

"Okay," Claire said, realizing that she'd pushed Sylvia about as far as she could for the time being. "But can you at least give me the contact information for Caroline's uncle and family?"

"How can I do that? Then they'd know for sure that I was talking about them!"

"This *is* a murder investigation, Sylvia. Don't you think that finding Caroline's killer is more important than worrying about the feelings of relatives who chose to leave her to the mercy of the foster care system after her parents died? Besides," Claire went on "the police could have found their names in an address book when they searched the apartment. I can ask them if you don't tell me."

"I don't have a phone number for them but their last name is the same as Caroline's—Hewitt—and her uncle's first name is Frank and, like I said, they live in Calgary. Now, I really have to go." And with that, Sylvia got up and quickly left the coffee shop without a backward glance.

Claire was not ready to leave, however. She got herself a second cinnamon roll and another cup of coffee, pulled a notebook and pen out of her purse and began making notes about the information she'd heard from Sylvia. As she worked, it became obvious that there were more questions yet to ask and she made a list of them for the next time she could get Sylvia alone to continue their talk.

Chapter 5: Claire Can't Resist

Claire had a dilemma. In the old days she would have kept all this new information to herself and gone off alone or with Tia to interview possible suspects. But she'd promised McCoy that she'd work with him this time. Also, she was a little more wary of the dangers she could face and had lost some of her past zest for jumping into unknown situations. But in the end that didn't stop her.

Claire did phone Inspector McCoy to tell him about the uncle, aunt and cousin in Calgary. He was grateful for the information and promised to follow up on it. "There was no next of kin listed in her wallet or in the gym personnel file but I should be able to track them down with the information you've provided," he said.

"Could you let me know if you find them, please?" Claire asked. But what she didn't mention was that she'd also heard about the ex-boyfriend and had contact information for him. She reasoned to herself that she wasn't going to hold it back for long, just long enough to visit him first herself!

The following Saturday, she arose at her usual time and helped her assistant get 15 year-old Jessie ready for a trip to the newly re-opened Royal Alberta museum in downtown Edmonton. After wandering around for a bit they would have lunch there and Claire had asked them to bring her back two of the delicious butter tarts on offer in the new cafeteria.

When Jessie heard the DATS bus (Disabled Adult Transportation System) lowering the lift and realized that Claire wouldn't be going with them she made a loud complaining sound to indicate her disappointment. Claire hugged her and explained that (once again) she had important things to do and Jessie and Ellen would have to go without her.

When they were safely on the bus and it was pulling away, Claire closed the door. She sat down at her kitchen table for a second cup of coffee and, not for the first time, contemplated the notion that she should never have been a mother—and certainly not to someone with such high needs as Jessie. *I'm too self-centered, too busy taking care of my own wants and needs to nurture anyone else,* she thought sadly. But Claire had limited time for self-recrimination if she was going to complete the task she'd set herself for the day.

Dan had gone off for his regular Saturday morning run so she was free to act. Claire picked up the phone and dialed the number she'd located for Caroline's ex-boyfriend. Sylvia had not been quite sure about the spelling of his last name but according to the on-line Edmonton phone directory there was only one Alexandru Grozavu.

"Hello, who *is* this?" was the curt greeting when the phone was picked up.

Claire took a deep breath and went into her prepared speech. "Hi, am I speaking to Alexandru?"

"Y-e-s. Who wants to know?"

"I'm a friend of Caroline's and my gym trainer told me that she was recently murdered. I was really upset but we haven't been in touch lately and I don't know what was going on in her life. My trainer told me that you were her boyfriend so I thought maybe I could talk to you—and you could help me understand how something like this could happen," Claire finished limply.

"Who *are* you again?"

"My name is Ophelia Bur...quist," Claire replied, adding a syllable to her last name on the spur of the moment. Actually, I am—or was—more of a friend of her mother but I knew her quite well when she was growing up and I recently moved to the city and I thought I would try to look her up. I just happened to ask my trainer if she'd ever heard of her and that's when she told me. It's so shocking!" Claire babbled.

"Well, I can't help you. We broke up some time ago."

From the cold, impatient tone of his voice, Claire was quite sure he was about to hang up so she quickly interjected. "Wait, please, if I could just have a few minutes of your time so you could tell me what she was like when you knew her, what she was doing, what she was into. I just need to understand. She had such a nice family. I just don't understand how this could happen."

"Sorry, I have an appointment later this morning so now's not a good time."

"Please ... I looked up your address and I could be there in 20 minutes, 15 even. Could I please just talk to you for a few minutes? I'm so upset. I can't focus on anything else until I get some understanding."

There was silence at the other end of the phone and Claire waited tensely for a response. Finally, Alexandru replied grudgingly. "Okay, I guess, but it'll have to be short—15 minutes tops. I've got things to do."

"*Thank* you, thank you!" Claire replied, her voice oozing gratitude. She hung up the phone, grabbed her purse and practically hurled herself out the door, the piece of paper with his number and address clutched in her hand. Only when she was six blocks away did she realize that she had not left a note for Dan to tell him where she had disappeared. *Oh, well,* she said to herself. *I'll tell him later.* This was not the first time she'd had occasion to utter those words!

The door was opened by a muscular but somewhat overweight man about 5'10" and with shoulder-length dark, greasy hair. He lounged in the doorway looking at her until Claire announced her name and asked if she might come in. He moved aside and pointed to a sofa in an adjoining room. Then he parked himself in a huge lounge chair that placed his rather aromatic stocking feet only a short distance from Claire's face. She cleared her throat nervously and opened her mouth to speak but he interrupted her before she could start.

"Let's get on with it," he growled. "Like I said, I don't have much time."

"How did you meet, Caroline—and when?" Claire asked.

"I met her last April about this time. I knew a friend of hers from work, Laura, and she introduced us." We started going around together soon after that—until she ditched me a couple of months ago."

"Do you know why?"

"Oh, she concocted some story about me being *'abusive'* to her but I don't see how what passed between us could be called abuse."

"What *did* she complain about?"

"She didn't like the way I talked to her in front of others. She said it was *patronizing!* And then ... I may have slapped her around a little a couple of times—but I *needed* to! She would get out of control, all hysterical-like. And then she would do something stupid like spend a whole bunch of money on clothes.

"Well, you weren't living together, were you? She wasn't spending *your* money, was she?"

"No...but if we were going to have any kind of future together I needed to work that out of her. It was for her own *good!"*

Claire winced inwardly but then talked quickly to keep the conversation going. She was aware that the time he'd agreed to allot to her was passing rapidly. "Some people are quite immature and that can be very frustrating. It's hard to deal with them, to help them to see that sometimes their behavior is self-defeating."

"Yeah, that's right!" he replied, with almost a note of gratitude in his voice. "She was immature and didn't know what she was doing. I needed to help her to see— because I cared about her. But all I got was a slap in the face and she ditched me. And she wasn't even satisfied with *that!* She told Laura and Laura told our boss—*her* version of it. He called me on it and I explained it to him just like I explained it to you. But he wasn't satisfied with that and he fired me. He said he couldn't have people with *'anger management issues'* working for him. Something could happen and he could get sued if I ever got out of control like that with a customer."

"Oh, that's *terrible!"* Claire responded in a commiserating tone. "What kind of work were you doing? Did you have a union that could have gone to bat for you?"

"Huh? No. I was a bouncer. I worked in a *bar!"*

Claire blinked in surprise but then continued smoothly. "Well, I would imagine that you *need* those kinds of skills to do that job successfully."

"Ya *think?* That's what I told him. But he mentioned a coupla incidents that had happened before. Nothin' too serious. Just one guy got a broken nose and another *said* he had a cracked rib. But they were really being obnoxious! What was I supposed to *do?"*

Claire nodded sympathetically but made no other response. She needed to get the conversation back on Caroline. "Did you see Caroline at all after you broke off with her?"

"No ... well, I might have cruised by her house coupla evenings just to see what she was up to. I figured she was hot into some other guy and that's why she dumped me. *You* know."

Claire nodded her head wisely, while thinking to herself: *Actually, I don't know. I don't know anything about the world you appear to be living in.* What she said was, "Yes, I suppose that's a very real possibility. Did you ever see her with anyone?"

"No, but that doesn't mean anything. I only drove by a few times and maybe looked in her windows coupla times but I wasn't lucky. I didn't catch her."

"Did the police visit you yet—ask you where you were when she died or if you saw anybody else lurking around there when you drove by?" Claire held her breath while she waited for an answer. She just had not known how else to ask it.

"No... wait! I had nothing to do with Caroline's murder. Like I told you, I only went around her house at night, usually after work, and I only ever went to the gym once to pick her up after work. I don't even remember where it is. Besides, the paper says it happened in the morning, not at night ... and no, I never saw nobody else when I drove by."

"And Caroline never talked to you about anyone ... anyone who might have had a grudge against her?"

"No. Well she did mention a coupla women at work. She said they were jealous of her, resented how she got all the new customers."

"Did she give you any names?"

"Just first names—Ellie and Sheri-Lu or Lyn or something."

"She never talked to you about her family or her school days—if there was anybody there, from her past, who might have it in for her?"

"No. Anyway, her parents are dead. She did mention some relatives in Calgary somewhere. Forest Lawn, I think she said. That's all I know."

"So nobody then?"

"Nobody. Now could you leave, please? I have to get going!"

"There's just one more thing. "*I* am not going to tell the police," Claire declared, lying smoothly. "But Caroline did talk about you at the gym from what I hear so somebody else is likely to mention you to them. You should get your alibi straight for when they track you down."

For the first time, Alexandru's bully-like demeanor shifted and he looked a little frightened. "Yeah, I guess I better do that. You sure you won't tell?"

"No. I got on their wrong side once before for interfering in a police investigation and I have no desire to go through that again. So, if they come, promise me that *you* won't mention I was here. That could get me in serious trouble for withholding relevant information in a criminal investigation from the police."

"Don't you worry about *that! I'm* not about to share information with the cops—not after the way they treated me after those two incidents at the bar happened!" Claire left then, feeling quite pleased with herself.

Chapter 6: The Good, the Bad, and the Ugly

The next Tuesday morning Claire phoned McCoy after she got to work to tell him about the ex-boyfriend and give him the contact information. "And who did you hear this from?" he snarled. "That same 'secret' source?"

"Sorry!" Claire responded cheerfully. "If you want me to keep looking for information at the gym I cannot let on that I'm in the pocket of the police." Claire added, "There are some there who don't seem to like you people very much," implying that her informant was one of them and that perhaps she had something quite unrelated to Caroline that she would rather keep hidden.

"I guess you're right," he growled. "Just be careful and don't go snooping around by yourself!"

"Yes and yes," Claire replied, with her fingers crossed behind her back. She hung up the phone and went to the bathroom where she threw up the burrito she had had for breakfast. *I shouldn't have had that,* she said to herself, *but it seemed like the right thing to do at the time.*

"Claih, Claih. We go Nine Haggy now?" Roscoe was calling her and she wiped her face and put on a smile before exiting the bathroom. They needed to leave shortly for an 11 o'clock art class at the Nina Haggerty Gallery, a special place that catered to the artistic needs and interests of people with cognitive disabilities.

"Good. You're all ready, Roscoe! I just have to grab my stuff and we'll be off."

Claire thought about correcting his highly butchered enunciation but knew it was a hopeless task beyond his control. Roscoe's underdeveloped jaw, a common characteristic of individuals with Down Syndrome, made moving his tongue into the correct position in his mouth to make the required speech sounds difficult to impossible. In order to even talk, he and others in his situation tended to seek out various shortcuts so they could circumvent the most difficult tongue positions. This made communication difficult and, perhaps even worse, signaled to others that they were less intellectually capable than they actually were.

The class at the gallery lasted an hour and Roscoe really appeared to enjoy it. Afterward, he wanted to remain there and practice the new technique he had been learning about creating perspective, by drawing the outlines of a line of houses on a street. Claire tried to be patient but was still feeling queasy. She was afraid she would have to throw up again so after another half-hour she signaled to Roscoe that they needed to leave. He put his supplies away grudgingly and she was sorry to disappoint him.

"You need to check out your clothes for your shift at the restaurant tonight, Roscoe," Claire reminded him. Three nights a week Roscoe worked as the Maître 'd at the *Three Musketeer's Restaurant.* Technically, the restaurant belonged to Roscoe because it had been compensation for the grief he had suffered after various attempts had been made on his life. However, his mother liked to act like it belonged to her and she dealt with a good chunk of the profits accordingly, much to Claire's disgust.

In any case, Roscoe enjoyed his work at the restaurant, welcoming people and ushering them to their places. Claire had coached him to say, "Welcome to Woscoes" since 'r's were beyond him and the actual restaurant name was way beyond him. His mother did not like this but then she did not like the restaurant name he had chosen either, which was a nod to himself and his two roommates at the 'co-op', as Claire and the rest of their support group referred to the home they shared.

After they got back to the house, Claire made them both a cup of tea and she felt somewhat better. *But I really must make time to see the doctor,* she told herself, worrying that she might have stomach cancer or maybe a parasite. At that point in her ruminations her cell phone rang and it was Inspector McCoy. "We tracked down the boyfriend and brought him in," he said tersely. "I think he might be good for it—but then you already know that, don't you? He mentioned your name at one point. And then he said, 'Oh, I wasn't supposed to say that!' I don't think he's too bright."

"Oh, I see," Claire said weakly. Just then she heard the DATS bus arriving and watched as the driver unloaded Mavis in her wheelchair, while Bill stood beside him guarding her jealously and repeating the mantra he always used when this was happening. "*I* do, *I* do!"

"You agreed you weren't going to interfere. You have compromised his testimony!" McCoy went on.

At that point, Claire decided she had nothing to lose and she might as well say what she thought. "I don't believe he did it. He's a bully and not the sharpest knife in the drawer, like you say, but the story he told was consistent and at no point did he contradict himself or appear to be prevaricating."

"Well, we'll never know that, will we, since you had the first crack at him and he had plenty of time to refine his story before we got to him!"

I really shouldn't lie and be sneaky, Claire told herself sternly. *I am so bad at it!* But just then there was a knock at the door and she excused herself to answer it. "Mavis and Bill are at the door, just back from their program. I need to let them in and assist them with getting their outer clothes off," she told McCoy. He said a curt good-bye and she hung up the phone gratefully.

Later at home she pondered the situation as she prepared supper for Jessie and Dan and herself. She needed to do something to redeem herself in McCoy's eyes, but what? He certainly wasn't going to share any information he might uncover at this point! And there did not seem to be any other leads to follow up. *What to do?*

The next day Claire headed to the gym before work and this time she walked around the space considering what she remembered about the day Caroline had been murdered. Then it hit her. There *was* something. *One* possibility. But in her role of frightened new member she couldn't ask the front desk person the question she needed to ask. However, she knew somebody who could—Sylvia.

Claire saw Sylvia near the exercise table talking to Gladys, the supervisor. She hastily wrote a note and folded it into her hand. Then she walked towards the table and stood there hesitating. They both noticed and Sylvia walked towards her.

"I don't know if I dare try again or not," Claire said timidly.

"Here, let me help you up there," Sylvia offered. Claire clutched at Sylvia's hand for support and in the process slipped her the note. Sylvia raised her eyebrows in surprise but once she had Claire safely on the table she casually stuck her hand in her pocket.

"Thank you!" Claire said, loud enough for the supervisor to hear. "And thank you again for calming me down the other day. It really helped."

"No problem," Sylvia replied. "By the way, have you decided to reregister for sessions yet? If you *are* planning to do so, it would be good to do it soon. There's a promotion on right now and training sessions are $5.00 off if you buy 24 or more but I don't know how long that deal will last." Again, Sylvia spoke a little louder than necessary for the supervisor's benefit.

Later, after ordering their coffees at Starbucks, Claire sat at a small table near the back and waited. Sylvia arrived shortly. She sat down and thanked Claire for the coffee. "Okay, what do you want me to do?" she asked.

"Who do you know best at the front desk?"

"Marcie. But she's not in today. She should be back tomorrow."

"Can you ask her if any of the repair or maintenance men have keys? Their presence has to be announced every time they're in the building so I imagine that lengthy repairs might have to be done after hours when they won't be making any of the women who wear hijabs uncomfortable, having to stay covered up while they're exercising. And if they had to do bathroom repairs during operating hours that would be difficult for everyone."

"Okay, I'll ask Marcie tomorrow. But there's something else. Two or three months ago, we started having problems with the air conditioning system here and a company was hired to fix it. Their workers were in and out a lot of times trying to deal with the issue. They would be up on the roof but every time they came down onto the main floor to get something or to leave they had to phone the front desk first so their presence could be announced in advance. It was a big hassle for them and there was lots of complaining. And after this went on for about a month, they finally decided the system was too old to be fixed and needed to be replaced."

"What happened then?" Claire asked.

"They brought in the new system and lugged it up there but the only part of the gabled roof that's flat is right over the women's change room and that's where it had to be placed. They had to have continual access to the change room while they worked because of the wiring issue so they started working nights. This has gone on and on and I'm not sure if they're finished yet. I haven't seen them around lately but they could have been here still at the time Caroline died."

"Would Marcie know?"

"Probably."

"Would she know if they had their own key?"

"I'll ask her tomorrow."

Claire changed the topic then. "I *did* see that Alexandru guy that Caroline was dating," she said, and she shared some of their conversation. "Unfortunately the police inspector found out about my advance visit when he came and was very annoyed. He thinks that Alexandru is the murderer and that, by seeing him first, I gave him time to set up an alibi."

Sylvia looked surprised. "I don't think he can be the murderer ... not the way Caroline talked about him. She was more annoyed by him than afraid."

"She *did* tell her friend that he was abusing her and as a result Laura told his boss and got him fired."

"But Caroline never thought that would happen. She just wanted to create a little heat for him so he'd leave her alone."

"He admitted himself that he abused her—although he didn't call it that. He said he had to teach her a lesson."

"She told me that he grabbed her wrists and shook her a couple of times, and once he slapped her when he got upset by the way she was spending her money so freely. He told her he wanted to help her live right; that he hoped they'd have a future together and they needed to be on the same page about how money was spent. But she really didn't see him as an abuser. She just wasn't interested in him after a while but he kept lurking around and that was what was annoying her. I met him once when she had him pick her up from work because her car was in the garage. I don't think he's all that bright."

"I wondered about that myself," Claire admitted. "And after he agreed not to mention my visit to the police he accidentally blabbed, anyway. Not only that! He went on to say 'Oh! I wasn't supposed to say that!' Who *does* that?"

Sylvia grinned. "I guess he got *you* in hot water."

"Yes. And I need something to get me back in McCoy's good books."

Chapter 7: How to Put Your Problems in Perspective

It was Friday morning and Claire woke up nauseated again. This time she decided that she really had to deal with the issue and she phoned her doctor and got an 11 o'clock appointment. Then she made arrangements for a substitute at the co-op. By the time she'd showered and dressed, Jessie had left for school. Dan had agreed to get her ready since Claire wasn't well and she noted that Jessie's pink lunch pail was still in the fridge.

"I couldn't find it," Dan explained, "so I made her another one."

Claire said nothing but wondered how he would manage on his own if whatever she had was 'terminal'.

Once Claire arrived at Dr. Clandonald's office, the receptionist directed her toward the weigh scale and Claire discovered, much to her disgust, that she had put on another two pounds. She was then asked for a urine sample and once that was produced Claire was ushered into the examining room. The doctor arrived shortly after and asked various questions while doing some poking and prodding around her abdominal area. Then he asked her when her last period was.

"Oh, I can't even remember. They've been irregular for some time. I suppose I am in pre-menopause now that I'm in my forties."

There was a knock at the door and the nurse handed him a paper referring to the results of the urine sample. Claire watched anxiously as he looked at it but he didn't seem upset. Dr. Clandonald turned to her and smiled. "Well, I think I know why you've been having all those nausea attacks. You are pregnant!"

Claire was stunned. "That can't be!" she croaked. "I was told when Jessie was born that I wouldn't be able to have any more children—and Jessie is 15 now!"

"Well, whoever told you that was wrong because you're definitely pregnant. The problem is that I don't know how many weeks or months you are because of your faulty memory. I'm going to send you for an ultrasound test right now, Stat. Pregnancy at your age involves a higher degree of risk than normal and the sooner we know how far along you are the better. Just wait here while I make the arrangements. Are you driving? If may have to be at a clinic further away."

"Yes... but wait! Aren't you going to check me for stomach cancer? I have all the symptoms according to the Google site I checked!"

"We will do complete blood work and a second, more thorough urine test but I think it's safe to say that all the symptoms you have reported, including your weight gain, can be explained by your pregnancy. I'll know more once I get the results of the ultrasound. Please make an appointment with the receptionist when you leave but wait here until I arrange for the ultrasound and give you the requisition for that and for the other tests.

Claire sat in stunned silence. To say that this changed everything was an understatement. *What will Dan say?* she thought. *Will he be happy or will he resent the fact that there will be still more childcare work to do?* She didn't even know how she felt, apart from feeling stunned. She did a quick mental calculation. *I'll be sixty by the time he or she graduates from high school!*

It was ten minutes before the doctor returned and then it was to discover that she had a half-hour drive ahead of her. *Should I call Dan now or should I wait to tell him in person?* She decided on the latter, made the doctor's appointment for a week hence and left the clinic.

By the time Claire got home, it was three in the afternoon. She had stopped for lunch since she felt too hungry to wait until she returned. Dan was not there and the phone message light was blinking. Dan. He was in a meeting and would be home later, probably between 5 and 5:30. Claire phoned back but he didn't answer so she left a message herself. "I'll meet you at Sorrentino's. I will make the appointment for 5:30."

Claire sat back and wondered what to do. *Should I call Tia? No. Dan has the right to know first!* She put on the kettle but then decided against it. Always one for action, she grabbed her coat and went out to the car, planning to head for the nearest big bookstore. *I should go to Audrey's,* she thought. *Support our local bookstore.* But the staff there knew her and she was more likely to run into other people she knew there than elsewhere. *No. I'll go to Chapters. And it's closer anyway—straight down Calgary Trail.*

In less than ten minutes, she was there and found a parking spot nearby reserved for 'mothers-to-be'. She pulled in and patted her stomach but her mood soured when a young woman passing by gave her a suspicious look. Inside the store it didn't take long to find the relevant section and she began reading avidly. However, there were many books to choose from and she couldn't make up her mind. If she'd been at Audrey's she would have been able to receive some helpful advice but a survey of the young women 'sales associates' didn't fill her with confidence. Finally she spotted an older clerk and timidly asked her what she would advise.

"Is it for you or for your daughter?" the woman asked, but in such a tone that Claire didn't take offence.

"It's for me," Claire acknowledged. "I just found out. My daughter is fifteen!" she blurted.

"Congratulations!" the woman said warmly. "What a happy surprise! Are you excited?"

Claire talked then, all the pent up feelings coming out. She told her about Jessie and about being told she could never have more children. She told her about how she had only just started searching out a new career path a few years earlier, after all her extended years of childcare, and she described what she'd been doing with Roscoe and Mavis and Bill, and about the home she had developed for them.

The woman listened patiently, responding from time to time with interest and encouragement. There were few customers in the store at that point on a Friday afternoon. Finally she asked, "Are you happy about this pregnancy, or sad?"

"I don't know!" Claire said. "I'm still in shock!"

"Are you considering termination?"

Claire looked at her, startled. "Never! Unless, what if it's like Jessie?"

"Is Jessie's condition genetic?"

"No, but…"

"Well, then, why *should* it be? Why should your baby be at any more risk than other babies?"

"Well, the doctor did say it would be a high risk pregnancy."

"They only say that because of your age. What are you? Forty?"

"Forty-two," Claire acknowledged.

"So? I had my last when I was 45 and she's fine. She's 15 now, same age as your daughter. She's on the honor roll in high school and her plan is to be a veterinarian. She loves animals, particularly cats."

Claire remembered her promise to Sylvia and said to herself *I must keep this woman in mind if my other plan for a home for Fergus doesn't work out.*

They talked a bit more and the woman helped her to select three books she thought would be the most useful. Claire would have kept on talking; it was so good to have someone to share this news with. But more customers had come into the story and the woman excused herself. However, Claire got her name, Mary Hart, and her business card. Mary invited her to call if ever there were other issues around the pregnancy Claire would like to discuss. And then she was off.

Claire looked after her fondly. *I am so glad that happened,* she said to herself—and then she glanced at her watch. To her horror she discovered that it was already 5:10 and she hadn't made it through the cash yet. Fortunately, the line-up was short and she was soon on Gateway Boulevard for the ten-minute drive to the restaurant. Only then did she realize that she hadn't made the reservation and it was a Friday night.

Claire walked nervously into the restaurant and explained to the person who greeted her that she didn't have a reservation. "That's okay," she was told cheerfully. We have one table left!" It was not the best table exactly, being adjacent to the washrooms, but Claire thought that would have its advantages. Bladder frequency was another problem that she'd been experiencing lately.

She had only just sat down when Dan joined her. He raised his eyebrows at the table and Claire explained that this was all that had been available. She didn't mention that she'd only secured it five minutes previously. Her lack of foresight on various issues was a bone of contention in their lives together!

"What's the occasion?" Dan asked.

"Do we need an 'occasion' to go out to dinner once in a while?" Claire asked.

"What did the doctor say?"

"I'm pregnant," Claire said rather flippantly—because she didn't really know how else to say something like this.

"You're joking, right?"

"No," she said in a small voice. "It's true."

Dan just stared at her. The server came to ask them what they'd like to drink but he waved her away. A full minute passed before he could even speak. "You're sure?" he croaked. "How far…"

"The doctor doesn't know. He sent me for an ultrasound today. I'll find out when I see him again in a week."

"I don't know what to say," he began weakly. "What if …?"

"I know."

Such horrible heartbreak they had had. Such a struggle to make the best out of the shattered remains of what could have been. So much work! She looked up and saw the tears in Dan's eyes. What if it turned out to be the same thing again? But what if it didn't? Then she felt the tears in her own eyes … tears of joy—and bewilderment.

"What are you thinking?" she asked.

"I *love* Jessie but there's so much we can't share with her. What would it be like to share our world, our tastes, our interests, our hobbies, our values—even our prejudices with our own child?"

"I guess that is about what I am thinking," she replied, half-crying and half-laughing. The server came then to give them menus but Dan stood up.

"I think maybe we won't be staying after all. I'm sorry for the misunderstanding." Claire meekly followed him out the door without a backward glance.

Back home, they checked on Jessie and talked to her assistant for a few moments about Jessie's day. Then Claire put a frozen pizza in the oven. When it was ready, they took it and some glasses of juice to their bedroom to eat in private. But they had to force themselves to attend to the pizza before it got cold. Eating was just not top of mind for either of them.

"What will you do about your work?" Dan asked Claire. "You've enjoyed it so much. You waited so long to do something that engaged your interests beyond just looking after Jessie all the time."

"That's true but ... I don't know. Lately I've been feeling restless. It's not that I don't want what I have developed with the three of them to continue. It's just that I don't necessarily want to do the work involved any more. If I can find somebody really good to take over, I won't actually be sorry to give it up."

"That's a big if though, isn't it?"

"I don't know. I can imagine that there's somebody out there who could care about them the way I do and be able to think up new possibilities to keep their lives as rich and interesting as possible and still manage to stay organized which, as you know, is not one of my strengths. It might work out even better. And it's not like I would just back off altogether. I would still be around to make sure I approved of what was happening and to make program suggestions when needed."

Dan looked at her fondly. "I guess you would at that".

"And," Claire went on, "in this new baby book I was reading today it mentions how easy it is for new mothers to become isolated. Well, I have a built-in community. The baby and I can go there and to Tia's house and her parent's house and Amanda's place and even to visit Hilda and her animals. They will all appreciate the visits!"

"What about baby stuff? You gave all the things we bought for Jessie away."

"I'm sure Tia will lend me what she bought for Marion when she outgrows it. I know Tia and Jimmy are not planning for any more. And if we have a girl we won't have to worry about dressing her for the next 10 years. She can just wear Marion's cast-offs!"

"You haven't told her yet, have you?"

"No. I wanted you to be the first to know."

Chapter 8: Claire Gets Another Shock

The next morning, Claire called Tia from work to arrange a get-together. Tia was also at work and could only talk for a minute. She suggested they grab a coffee after they both finished for the day.

"No, I need more of your time than that. Dan is leaving for another business meeting tomorrow morning. Could you possibly arrange things so you could sleep over here tomorrow night? I'll make us a quick supper and we will have a good catch-up. I have a new mystery to tell you about for one thing!"

"I'll talk to Jimmy tonight and let you know. It depends if he and Mario are willing to look after Marion. I know Amanda has plans for that evening." Their 75 year-old neighbor, Amanda, was the person who looked after 16-month old Marion when Tia was at work at the hospital during the weekdays.

"Okay," Claire responded. "I'll tentatively arrange evening coverage for Jessie tomorrow until she goes to bed."

Tia arrived at 6 the next evening after going home from work to arrange supper, spend some time with Marion and put everything in place for her care for the evening. *A woman's work is never done*! Tia muttered to herself. But for once, Jimmy didn't complain about taking over with Marion because he knew that Tia had had very little time to spend with her closest friend, Claire, in quite a while and that it was important that they have a good visit together now.

During supper, Claire told Tia about the murder and how her investigation was going so far. Tia stiffened a bit when Claire mentioned the role that Sylvia was playing in helping her this time around but they both knew that life had a way of moving on. Circumstances change, priorities change and therefore relationships have to change over time. Claire smiled at her half apologetically, knowing, as did Tia, that the special friendship they shared would always be there.

After supper, they retreated to the special sitting area Claire had set up in the basement level of their bungalow so she and Dan could have their own private space when an assistant was caring for Jessie.

"There's something else I need to talk to you about, Tia", Claire said, just as Tia had opened her mouth to speak.

"Yes, what is it?" Tia asked, with a note of patience in her voice.

"Claire took a deep breath and then made her big announcement. "I'm pregnant!"

Tia stared at her stupidly and said nothing for a minute. Finally, she stuttered, "But I thought—you told me—how did this happen?"

This was not the response Claire had been expecting and she sat back, feeling deflated.

Tia saw this and quickly added, "I'm very happy for you and Dan, Claire," and she gave her a hug.

"Well, you don't *seem* that happy. I thought you would be thrilled for me."

"I *am*. It's just. I was waiting to tell *you* something!"

"*What?*" Claire said sourly. "Did you get another promotion?" She was thinking of all the times she'd wanted to share something with Tia but couldn't during the past year since Tia had been working full time in her position as supervisor of housekeeping at the hospital.

"No," Tia replied evenly. "I'm also expecting."

It was Claire's turn to look shocked, and suddenly she started laughing. "Well, there goes my plan for bumming baby clothes and equipment off you!" she said cheerfully. "I was just reassuring Dan that we wouldn't have to worry about any of that. I guess we will have to consider crowd-funding!"

Tia laughed, too, and Claire grabbed her and hugged her hard. "Do you know what this means? Our children will be growing up together. They will be best friends, just like you and me!"

"What if they don't like each other?" Tia said teasingly. For the next hour, they talked cozily about all things baby. Claire showed Tia the books she had purchased and Tia talked about homemade baby food recipes. But as this conversation was winding down, Tia turned to Claire and said, "Are you going to have the tests?"

"Tests?" Claire asked defensively.

"*You* know, Claire. Because of your age?"

"Oh, you mean for Down Syndrome and other possible genetic disorders?"

"Yes."

"Well, I haven't discussed it yet with Dan."

"What if…?"

If anybody else had asked this, Claire would have taken offence. But Tia knew all too well what Claire had gone through with Jessie so there was no point in pretending that this was not a serious issue for Claire and Dan to be considering.

"I don't know what I'd do to tell you the truth," Claire replied. "Even someone with Down syndrome would function a lot higher than Jessie does. Look how great Roscoe is?" But after a pause, she went on, speaking in a wistful tone. "It would just be so wonderful to have a normal child, somebody I could share with mentally on every level, somebody I could help develop who actually had significant potential to develop. In fact, I don't think I could go through all the work I have done with Jessie for so little gain again! Please pray for us, Tia! Pray it won't happen again!"

"I will, every day—and Jimmy and Mario will, too. I can promise you that! But I have had my own reason to check the statistics. The odds of Down syndrome increase by maternal age and even at 35 they're about 3 times higher than at age 20. I don't know what they are at your age, Claire."

"I looked it up today," Claire replied. "One report on line said that 40 year old women have a 1 in 84 chance of producing a child with Down syndrome."

"Wow!" was all Tia could say.

"Well, I'm seeing the doctor again next week. He sent me for an ultrasound and we'll have the results then as to how far I am along. And I'll be asking him about genetic testing," Claire said grimly.

They changed the subject then. It was getting just too frightening. Their old intimacy had returned and Claire finally had the confidence to tell Tia about the strange interaction that had occurred between her and Inspector McCoy. She braced herself for Tia's response, but once again that evening she was in for a surprise.

"Well, it was only a matter of time," Tia replied calmly. "His attraction to you has been quite obvious for anyone who cared to notice."

"*I* never noticed!" Claire declared.

"That figures, Claire. You have a lot of strengths but you are not particularly observant!"

Claire said nothing for she knew that what Tia said was true in general. But it wasn't entirely true that she had not noticed McCoy's change in attitude towards her! She just hadn't put it into words to herself.

"Well," Tia went on. "You've raised several problems: who is the murderer? How do we find him? And what was McCoy's past romantic life like and how do we help him find true happiness in the present so he will stop mooning over the unattainable you?"

Claire responded to the latter challenge first since that was the one that had a certain sting in it. "Are you suggesting we look for somebody for McCoy who will be even better than me so he can cast me aside?" she asked half jocularly.

"More or less, Claire," Tia said dryly. "And get over it! It's not that much of a compliment. The man obviously has problems!"

"You're just jealous that he fixated on me rather than you when you're the younger, thinner, prettier one!"

Tia regarded her friend with a certain degree of compassion. She knew that all Claire's joking around was designed to cover up the fact that she generally didn't feel that positive about herself, particularly her physical self. Apparently, McCoy's sudden romantic attentions had been a real jolt in the ego for her, even though they had at the same time created a moral dilemma. "Claire, listen to me. No good can come from this. Finding a way to divert his attention is the best course of action to help him. And the best way to help you with your own particular self-image problem is for you to keep working out at the gym and changing your eating habits. When do you see your new trainer again?"

"Tomorrow morning, as a matter of fact. I almost forgot. Thanks for reminding me. But how am I going to keep working out if I am pregnant? It might hurt the baby!"

"People do and I'm sure your trainer will know what you can and cannot safely do. *I* certainly plan to keep exercising. All the research I've read on exercise during pregnancy indicates that if done right it improves the health of both mother and baby because of increased oxygen flow, and makes delivery and subsequent recovery easier."

"Fine! Let's talk about something else. How are we going to track down the murderer if we're both pregnant? It's one thing taking chances on an injury or worse for ourselves but doing so for the baby is just off the table as far as I'm concerned!"

"Well, of course; that goes without saying. But you did say you have this Sylvia person. Do you think she's brave enough to do the leg work?"

"I don't know. She's kind of soft and timid looking if you know what I mean. And her name! Sylvia! People with guts generally have more assertive sounding names like … like *Jen* or *Gwen…or* uh *Blair.*"

"Or *Claire* maybe?" Tia asked dryly.

"Okay, *fine!* I get your point! I'll try to talk to her tomorrow about it but we have to be very discreet. We don't want anybody else to know about our connection. The most likely murderer is someone right there in that gym!"

They talked some more then, about their jobs and what they were going to do about them, given their changed circumstances, and how these new babies were going to change their lives. But by 10 p.m. they were both tucked into their respective beds in order to be sufficiently rested for the day ahead.

Chapter 9: Claire Passes the Torch

Before leaving for the gym the following morning, Claire sent a quick text to Sylvia. She knew that Thursday was her day off and hoped that she would be able to come over to the co-op so they could discuss the case further. Then she left for her session with Candace.

The trainer took the news of Claire's pregnancy very well and didn't seem to think it would make much difference to her program in the early stages. Candace explained that she would modify it as necessary as they went along. Claire expressed concern about raising her heart rate during the cardio workouts but Candace assured her that that was fine. She had kept up to date on the research and worked with a number of pregnant women in the past. As for the age factor, she didn't think it was significant. "You are basically healthy and that's what counts," she told Claire.

Although she was tired and winded by the time the workout finished, Claire did feel energized and that feeling lasted throughout the morning while working alternately with Roscoe and Bill who were both home that day. Claire hadn't expected Bill to be there but a last minute schedule change at the restaurant had made it necessary. She phoned Satou Boton, the head chef. He only worked during the three weekend evenings, and Claire asked him if Bill could come over for a visit since they had a close relationship. He readily agreed and Claire sent Bill off with a male assistant who had come in to take over the work with him at her request.

Claire needed both Bill and the assistant, Paul, to be gone before Sylvia arrived so they could have a private talk. Of course, Roscoe would be there and overhearing some of what they said but Claire didn't mind that. And she knew he wouldn't repeat it if asked not to. However, there was something she needed to tell him before then since it necessarily must come up in her conversation with Sylvia.

She had to tell him about the baby.

Once Bill and Paul were out the door, Claire asked Roscoe to sit down with her for a chat and a cup of tea. He was happy to leave his latest batch of math homework behind and oblige.

"Wha we talk abou, Claih?" he asked, as he contemplated his tea and wondered if he could sneak in a second spoon of sugar.

"I have something to tell you, Roscoe, some very happy news. I'm going to have a baby!"

Roscoe looked at her but said nothing.

"Aren't you happy for me, Roscoe?" Claire asked in a voice that was close to pleading.

There was another moment of silence and Claire could tell he was thinking things over. Finally he asked "Is Dan hoppy?"

"Yes, just like me!"

Again he was silent and Claire knew something was bothering him. Finally, he came out with it. "You maawy long time and no baby ....ony Jessie. Now you have baby?" Then Roscoe put his head down and asked in a voice that was almost inaudible. "Is *Dan* baby?"

Claire gasped. "*How* can you even *think* that, Roscoe?" Of *course,* it's Dan's baby ... my baby and Dan's baby ...our baby. She had automatically fallen into the teaching mode, repeating and rephrasing to clarify his understanding. But suddenly she realized why he had asked the question. "You *don't* have babies by *kissing!"*

"*Sauwy,* Claih. I hoppy for you."

"I understand why you asked. Inspector McCoy must be lonely. That's why he did that. I think we need to find him a girlfriend."

"He not nice. No guhl like him."

"There is somebody for everybody as the saying goes," she replied.

Roscoe looked sad when Claire said that, perhaps thinking of his own situation. But then he said, "Maybe your fwen who is coming, Sil? Silla?"

Claire looked thoughtful. "You just might have something there, Roscoe!" Roscoe smiled but just then the doorbell rang. Sylvia had arrived.

Claire introduced Sylvia to Roscoe and then Roscoe to Sylvia. This was a calculated ploy. She was also making the unspoken point to Sylvia that the three of them were on an equal footing.

Sylvia spoke in a high, slightly patronizing voice to Roscoe and slightly louder than necessary. Claire struggled to not comment and chalked it up to unfamiliarity on Sylvia's part with individuals challenged with Down syndrome. Instead she set about correcting this matter. "Roscoe and I were just discussing possible ways to proceed on finding the murderer and, as I have just shared with him, my personal situation has changed which will put me out of action. I'm afraid I'm going to need a point-man and I'm hoping you will be up for the job." Sylvia looked at her blankly. "I finally saw the doctor the day before yesterday," Claire went on. "As I told you, I've been having stomach problems. Well, it turns out I'm pregnant!"

Sylvia looked at her in horror. "Is it safe for somebody your age?" she blurted. Claire looked at her sourly and thought to herself, o*bviously, she has more than one misconception about other people!*

Claire replied smoothly and with just a hint of steel in her voice, "It should be fine! The …"

But at that point Roscoe broke in, *"Claih not ole … and she healthy …she go gym alla time now!*

Claire sat back and smiled happily. Her defender was back! She had missed his uncritical admiration of her after falling so precipitously in his esteem over the kiss debacle.

'The reason I asked you to come here today," Claire said, addressing Sylvia, is that this pregnancy changes everything. It's one thing for me to risk getting injured myself. But it's quite another thing to put the baby at risk and I cannot do that. You *did* say you wanted to help in any way you could. I'm still going to be sharing information with Inspector McCoy and he will be doing the potentially dangerous parts of the investigation but there are things I do that seem quite innocent at the time but sometimes get me into a spot of trouble. I can't take those chances now and I'm wondering if you are up for it—so we can bring Caroline's killer to justice?"

Sylvia said nothing and Claire went on, "In several of the cases McCoy and I have worked on together—or even when I've been working on them without his knowledge—it's what I've managed to uncover that finally led to the discovery of the murderer. And he would admit it, if pressed, in private …although he's always happy to take the credit in public."

"What kind of work are you talking about?"

"Oh, just what I've been trying to do in this case but can't do now, running down suspects and talking to them—or talking to others who know them or… occasionally… entering places where I might be able to uncover some clues."

"How do you do *that?*"

"Well sometimes the door is open—or maybe a window." After a pause, Claire added, "and I *do* have a set of lock picks." Sylvia looked horrified and Claire went on hastily. "Oh, I wouldn't expect *you* to use them! In a case like that, I would go with you and unlock the door and then I would stand guard while you went inside. That's how Tia and I used to do it."

"And if the police caught me?"

"Oh, that has happened to us a couple of times. McCoy was always involved and we were able to talk our way out of it."

"And if the criminals came back while I was inside?"

"You would hide—and we always wear dark clothes—and running shoes so we can get away fast. These kinds of operations we generally do at night."

At this point, Roscoe interjected, "You *b-a-d, Claih!* But there was a note of admiration in his voice.

Sylvia was shaking her head doubtfully. "You *did* say you wanted to find Caroline's killer?" Claire went on. "Well, just *wanting* doesn't get the job done. There is always some degree of risk involved but not generally a high risk. It's just enough that I can't participate directly while I'm pregnant. So are we going to catch this guy or *not?*"

Sylvia straightened her back. "I'm in—as long as it doesn't get too crazy. Where do we start?"

They talked strategy then and Claire asked Sylvia if she'd had a chance to talk to the receptionist about maintenance men access.

"Yes. She told me that their chief maintenance person, Stan Polansky, is the only one outside of the regular gym staff who has a key. He's a heating and plumbing specialist and if something goes wrong in either of those areas or if he has maintenance tasks to perform that need to be done outside of regular hours he needs to have direct access."

"Isn't there a security system? What about the code?"

"Yes, I asked about that—and, yes, he has the code."

"And did you ask about the air conditioning people?"

"Yes, they finished everything and were all gone at least two weeks before Caroline died."

"But how did they get in at night to work? Did they have their own key?"

"No. The arrangement was that Stan would let them in at night with his key and the door was set to lock automatically when they left in the morning."

"Well, I'm going to tell Inspector McCoy about him anyway—*and* about the air conditioning people. Just because Stan was supposed to let them in at night it doesn't mean that he didn't just loan them the key and tell them the combination one night because he couldn't be bothered being there when they arrived. He could have even left them with the key all week if they were working there every night and then they would have had a chance to get it copied!"

"Oh, I doubt that," Sylvia said primly.

"In this business you learn not to trust anybody," Claire replied. "Anyway, I'm going to tell all this to McCoy and that should go some way to getting me back in his good graces. But after he talks to this Stan person I'd like you also to talk to him. Do you know him at all?"

"Oh, yes. I've seen him around and we've exchanged a few words."

"Good! Okay, we'll leave that for down the road. Right now, the only other thing I can think of is to get into Caroline's apartment and see if we can find any information the police overlooked. Do you know where she lives?"

"Yes. She used to give me a key so I could water her plants and feed her cat whenever she was away on a short trip."

Claire held her breath. "Do you still have it?"

"As a matter of fact I do!" Sylvia said, surprised. "I had forgotten! Her last trip was recent and I didn't have a chance to return it to her before…." Her voice trailed off at the memory of the terrible event.

"Okay, that's where we'll start—and the sooner the better. I wish I knew if McCoy had managed to contact her Calgary relatives and if so, whether and when the cousin was coming to town."

"Well, there I *can* help you. Caroline's cousin called me yesterday, out of the blue! Apparently, Caroline had given her my contact information and told her if there ever came a time that her cousin couldn't reach her she should call me!"

"Well, why did she call now?"

"Apparently, she and her parents just returned from a three week European holiday that they'd been planning for a long time and they hadn't been following local news so knew nothing about Caroline's murder until Inspector McCoy called day before yesterday."

"Are they planning to come up here?"

"Just the cousin, Vanessa, is coming. She has to arrange to get the time off work so she wasn't sure how soon, but as soon as possible."

"Okay. We better do it tonight then. It could be our only chance."

"I do have plans" Sylvia began tentatively.

"Cancel them!" Claire barked. "This comes first!"

Sylvia looked a bit affronted but Roscoe just smiled. He was used to Claire becoming excited and bossy when she was onto something.

Chapter 10: Claire Just Can't Stay Out of It!

At 10 o'clock that evening, Claire and Sylvia met up in the alley behind Caroline's apartment building. Sylvia had parked nearby and Claire was a block away. That way if their presence was discovered and they had to leave immediately through the back door they could jump into Sylvia's car and escape. If, on the other hand, they could leave out the front unnoticed, then they could just sidle down the street to Claire's car, calmly drive over to where Sylvia's car was parked, and then both take off. Claire marveled at the steep learning curve of becoming a criminal. She had learned a lot in the past few years!

Caroline had provided Sylvia with a key to the back door of the building so that's how they entered. Despite her plan to remain behind as lookout, Claire changed her mind at the last moment. She reasoned that Sylvia could easily overlook an important clue since she had no expertise in what to look out for. They crept silently up the stairs to the third floor staying close to the edge of the steps so as not to alert anyone to their presence by a wayward creak. It was for that reason that they did not take the elevator—to avoid the telltale 'ding' of its arrival. Before leaving the stairwell, Claire handed Sylvia a pair of thin latex gloves to put on and she donned a pair as well.

Sylvia inserted the key in the lock and turned the doorknob carefully. Once inside, Claire headed directly to the glass balcony door through which a small amount of ambient light was coming. She turned its venetian blind slats upward to better shut out the faint light their penlights would produce and then opened the sliding glass door to check for quick exit possibilities should the need arise. A rope ladder was folded up neatly in the corner and she examined it. Apparently it could be thrown over the side and dropped to the ground to allow emergency exit in case of fire. Claire went back inside then but left the door an inch open. *I must remember to close it before we leave,* she reminded herself.

Claire pulled two small penlights from her purse and handed one to Sylvia, instructed her to always keep it pointed at the floor to avoid light escaping through the window. Claire checked each room systematically and Sylvia followed behind her, double-checking. In the small kitchen, Claire headed for the freezer at the top of the fridge and rooted around in any item there that was not factory sealed, but she found nothing. In the small desk in Caroline's bedroom she did find an old, outdated address book tossed in a drawer and apparently overlooked by the police in their previous search. She placed it in her purse. Meanwhile, Sylvia called Claire with her discovery. She had found a small key at the bottom of a vase of artificial flowers.

Just then they heard the ding of the elevator. Claire motioned Sylvia to follow her out onto the balcony and they had just exited when they heard voices outside the door. It sounded like Caroline's cousin had arrived early and was being allowed in, probably by the night manager.

Claire motioned for Sylvia to close the door while she quickly threw the rope ladder over the railing. She directed Sylvia to go first and followed quickly behind her, all the while worrying that Sylvia would panic and freeze. But that did not happen and once they hit the ground, they raced toward the gate at the back of the property. They had just made it through when the balcony door opened and the light from a flashlight arced around the yard. They crouched down behind the fence just before it reached them and heard voices as somebody discovered the hanging ladder.

Still squatting, they raced as best they could along the fence until they were beyond the flashlight's reach and then hurried towards the car. "Don't close the door completely; just latch it," Claire warned—and don't turn the lights on. Fortunately, the car was quite new and it started quietly. Sylvia eased it along the alley until they reached the corner and then she turned left, away from the apartment. At the next corner she corrected course and drove to where Claire's car was parked. "Go home now!" Claire hissed as she fumbled to get her keys out. "We'll talk tomorrow. Good job!" Sylvia just grinned at her in a dazed kind of way!

Most excitement she has had in a long time, I bet! Claire thought to herself—and then realized that her *own* heart was pounding.

The next morning she texted Sylvia early and asked if she could text back with a possible meeting time. "Please bring that key you found," Claire asked, before hanging up. Then she perused Caroline's old address book as she ate her breakfast. There were a few blank pages towards the end and, on the second to the last page, Claire found an enigmatic message that appeared to contain a code of some sort. The top line read B&T 21 and the bottom line read s-b 325. Claire pondered what that could mean but soon put it aside so she could get ready for work.

Later on in the morning, she was in the midst of going through some math corrections with Roscoe when the phone rang. It was Inspector McCoy. He wasted no time on preliminaries but announced that there had been a break-in the night before at Caroline's apartment. "Oh, really?" Claire replied, her voice squeaking slightly. "Maybe it was the murderer."

"We don't think so," McCoy replied, unless he—or *she* had a key."

"Maybe an ex-boyfriend?" Claire suggested weakly, noting his emphasis on the 'she'.

"Well, actually, we have a witness," McCoy drawled. "The old lady who lives next door to Caroline says she just happened to be up around eleven and saw two women sneaking across the yard. She says one looked young and on the thin side and the other was heavier and looked older—but 'not *really*' old, as she put it."

Snoopy old biddy! Claire said to herself bitterly. To McCoy she responded, "Well, then, all you have to do is track down any women who might have a key to Caroline's apartment."

"Oh, we have a line on that as well. This same woman heard Caroline talking to somebody she referred to as Sylvia about a month ago. Caroline was arranging for her to look after the cat and water the plants while she was away on a trip and to do that she would have had to have a key."

"The building supervisor might have let her in?"

"No, we checked."

Claire was sweating at this point, trying to figure out a way to get McCoy off Sylvia's track. "How do you know the person used a key? Was there any other possible way to get in?"

"Well, we know how they got out. There's a rope ladder that can be lowered from the balcony in case of fire."

"So maybe that's how they got in as well!" Claire suggested.

"No. As it happened, the building inspector had occasion to be on that side of the building late in the afternoon and there was no rope ladder hanging down then. And there would be no other way to access the apartment from the balcony otherwise."

Claire quietly banged the side of her head. She hadn't thought of that. The conversation ended then and she quickly called Sylvia. "I need to see you ASAP. Until then do *not* answer your phone!"

"What?"

"Not now. When can we meet and where?"

There was a short silence and then Sylvia responded, "I'll see you at Starbucks in 20 minutes. I'll take an early lunch break. Fortunately I don't have any more clients this morning. They all came in early."

"I'll be there," Claire said tersely, and hung up the phone.

When she arrived at the coffee shop, Sylvia was already there with a worried look on her face. Claire told her about the phone call and Sylvia regarded her reproachfully. "You told me that your plan was foolproof … that there was no way the police could involve me."

"I thought it was," Claire said wryly. "I just forgot that one little detail—about not being able to access the rope ladder from the ground."

"Well, what am I supposed to do when they come calling, which they will? They already know that Caroline and I were friends, according to what you just told me about that neighbor."

"How good are you at lying?"

"*Lying!* You want me to *lie* to the *police?*"

"Well," Claire said defensively. "It's not a crime to lie to the police …only if you're in court under oath."

"Oh, that's comforting!" Sylvia said sarcastically.

"Look! You're either going to have to say that you lost that key or that you gave it back—and whatever you say, they're going to then ask you for details.

That's why you have to prepare your story now and make sure you stick to it consistently!"

Claire was sitting facing the glass entry door and just then she saw two men in dark uniforms about to enter. "Get ready!" she hissed to Sylvia, and then she flitted down the hallway behind her to the washroom. Sylvia turned enough to see the policemen who were just inside the door by that time. She scanned the seat where Claire had been sitting but there was no evidence of her presence since she had not taken time to get a drink. Then she pulled out her sandwich and started nonchalantly eating it and scanning her phone at the same time. A tap on her shoulder startled her and she jumped involuntarily.

"Sorry to interrupt you, but could we have a moment of your time, please?' Sergeant Crombie asked smoothly. Since he and McCoy had interviewed her together previously there was no need for introductions.

"Of course" Sylvia replied, and she motioned to the chair at the table and a nearby, unoccupied one. Sergeant Crombie and Inspector McCoy sat down and introduced themselves. Twenty minutes later, they were gone and Sylvia headed for the washroom. She went directly to the sink and, with shaking hands, washed her face with cold water. Then she phoned the gym and explained that she was feeling ill and wouldn't be back for the rest of the day. She asked the receptionist to cancel her 3 p.m. appointment and gave her the contact information.

Claire crept out of the stall where she had lurked every time the door opened, and asked Sylvia how she was. "I feel horrible. I'm not even sure if I'm able to drive!"

"Look, Sylvia. Tia is home today because she had to take her daughter in for her regular check-up with the pediatrician this morning. Let's go over there and talk it out. We all need to be on the same page about this so I need to know exactly what you said to the police. I'll drive you and bring you back and maybe by that time you'll feel able to drive home."

"Okay," Sylvia said weakly. Claire called Tia to let her know that they were coming and that Sylvia was in pretty bad shape and then they left.

Tia was waiting for them with a pot of Earl Grey tea and some zucchini-chocolate chip muffins she had baked that morning. She settled Sylvia in a comfortable recliner in her living room with an afghan over her lap and a convenient pillow nearby. Then, she and Claire sat on the sofa opposite.

Claire updated Tia on the happenings of the night before, including her elaborate exit strategy and McCoy's unfortunate discovery of the female perpetrators. When she finished, Tia just sat back and laughed heartily. Sylvia looked confused and a little offended but Tia turned and said to Claire, after one last snicker, "Why is it, Claire, that the more clever and sneaky your plans are the more often they go wrong?" She turned back to Sylvia then and explained, "Claire is equally good at getting into trouble and getting out of trouble so tell me: How did she advise you to wiggle out of it *this* time?"

Sylvia just shook her head. *Who were these people anyway!* she wondered. But she carefully went over her interview with the police, trying not to leave anything out. Tia and Claire had both whipped out notepads and pens and were recording as she talked. "I pulled out my sandwich and cellphone and tried to look occupied when they arrived so they wouldn't be suspicious about me sitting there alone. They asked me about the key and I told them I'd given it back to Caroline at the gym after she got back from her trip—either the first time or the second time that I saw her there. I couldn't remember which but it would have been within that first week."

"Good detailing and keeping it flexible at the same time!" Tia said appreciatively.

Claire turned to Tia and said proudly, "See! She's turning into a mini-me!"

"Hopefully she won't be as good at getting into trouble as you are!" was Tia's rejoinder.

"They, of course, asked me if any one there had witnessed the exchange and I just said I didn't know but they could ask around," Sylvia interjected.

"Again, that was about as good an answer as you could give to such a question. You made it sound like you had nothing to hide," Tia said warmly.

"They seemed satisfied when they left but I don't *know,*" Sylvia concluded.

"They will most likely to be back," Claire warned, and they'll ask you the same questions in different ways just to see if they can catch you off guard. "Do *not* deviate from your story and do *not* add any more details. That's a sure way to get caught out!"

Tia had been busy writing on a small card as Claire talked and now she handed the card to Sylvia, along with a couple of blank ones. "Here, I've written down what you said. Go over it and make sure you've left nothing out and changed nothing. Then re-write it on another card exactly as it happened. Every morning, as soon as you get up, review it, and keep it with you in a hidden part of your purse so if they approach you again and you have a chance beforehand you can review it."

"It was a pretty simple story. Do I really have to go through all that rigmarole?"

"You would be surprised how quickly things can go wrong," said Claire darkly, speaking from experience. By the way, did you get a chance to speak to the maintenance man yet?"

"No, but he's supposed to be in tomorrow. I'll call you if I learn anything new," Sylvia said and shortly after that Claire and Sylvia left.

Chapter 11: The First Real Clue

The next morning, Claire took a deep breath and called Inspector McCoy at the office. He did not answer the phone and she was relieved. She left a message. "Hi, it's Claire. I just wanted to let you know that I found out about somebody else who has a key and the security code to the gym—a maintenance man named Stan Polansky. You might want to talk to him but I guess you don't want to let on to the people there that you have a mole feeding you information so you could just ask them if anybody other than the trainers has a key, maintenance people or cleaners maybe. Oh, there were also some workers from an air conditioning company coming in and out over the last couple of months to set up a new system. You might check how they were getting in. They had to do most of their work at night, apparently."

Claire was at work trying to get the tomato soup stain out of Roscoe's tux with his less than helpful assistance and at the same time closely monitoring the relationship between Mavis and a newly hired assistant. The task at hand was for Mavis to learn how to fit a foam square, diamond and rectangle into its matching foam board. Hal, the new hire, had been working with her for an hour and was getting nowhere. Both he and Mavis were clearly frustrated and Claire knew a change was in order.

"Hal, please get Mavis' jacket on. I'm taking her across the street for a visit with Tia and Marion. While I'm gone I'd like you to clean out the fridge and wash the kitchen floor. If you finish before I return, please fold the laundry in the drier and in the basket of clean clothes beside it. Roscoe, you sit at the kitchen table and do the rest of your math homework. If you get stuck you can ask Hal for assistance, okay?" Roscoe nodded grudgingly, although he would have much preferred to accompany Claire for the visit to Tia and Marion. Claire knew this and felt vaguely guilty—but she didn't want Roscoe in on her upcoming conversation with Tia.

It was Tia's day off and she had set herself a number of household tasks to do but she was happy to have company. However, Claire had a particular agenda item. Once they were settled and Mavis was engaged in watching Marion bounce around in her Jolly Jumper, Claire pulled the key Sylvia had discovered from her pocket and brought out Caroline's address book. She showed the code in the book to Tia and then showed her the key.

Tia looked at the key a long time, muttering to herself as she turned it from front to back. Finally, she looked at Claire. "There's something familiar about this key but I just can't remember what. Maybe it will come to me."

"Really?" Claire asked, feeling excited and hopeful for the first time. "Please try hard. We literally don't have anything else concrete to go on." After that, they drank tea and had a good visit. Their visits were all too rare these days.

Suddenly, Tia stopped in the middle of telling Claire a long story about Marion's latest escapade, pulling herself across the floor until she got to the kitchen garbage and managed to tip it over, and said, "I've got it…I've almost got it." She put her head in her hands and started humming to herself. Then she looked up.

"It's a bank! The Bal, Bomb...Balmoral! The Balmoral Bank and Tr ... Trust? Company, B & T!"

Claire stayed very quiet. "Where do you remember that from, Tia?" she asked.

Tia frowned. "It was sad, very sad ... something to do with a house. I was very small. Mamma and Papa were so upset. I remember that! Maybe Papa will remember more. I'll call him."

Since Tia's mother's assistant was in the home, her father Alberto was able to come over. However, before he came, he looked through a box of old papers where he stored a few special things he didn't want to part with when he'd moved to Edmonton from a farm in the Wetaskiwin area, 70 kilometers to the south. This had happened the year before because his wife Marissa had had the devastating stroke that had left her helpless.

Alberto arrived just a few minutes later since he and Marisa now lived next door. Once he settled down in the living room recliner and Tia had served him a cup of tea, he pulled from his pocket a key that matched the one Sylvia had found! The front was the same as Caroline's key but the back read s-b 247. Tia and Claire waited breathlessly for Alberto to tell them the story that went with it.

"When we arrived in Canada from Italy, we went first to Calgary where I had a friend. He got me a job and we lived in his basement for a year. You were born there, Tia. I recall that we had to replace the mattress on the bed. It got all stained with blood during the delivery." Alberto sat back and closed his eyes for a moment. He looked sad and Claire could imagine he was remembering difficult days but happier ones because he'd been sharing them with his beloved Marisa at a level he could no longer do.

"But what has the key to do with it?" Tia asked.

"Well, I'm coming to that. This friend, Mateo, got me a job working at the float glass factory where they made windowpanes for houses. It was hot work and dangerous if you didn't watch what you were doing. One guy there had burnt off two of his fingers! Anyway, Marisa and I were trying to save up for a house and Mateo convinced me to invest in this bank that was just starting up then." Alberto pulled out a piece of paper and read off the name: Balmoral and Truett. "We bought some shares and stored them at the bank in a safety deposit box we rented. It was the only security we had so that was all that was in the box. Well, one day we went there and the bank was closed. It had gone out of business and we read that the building itself was in foreclosure. I don't know what happened after that. We never went back and soon after that we moved to Edmonton where I got a better job working at the meat packing plant."

"So these keys are for safety deposit boxes but you don't know what happened to them or the building? Papa, may I have that paper you're holding and the key so I can look into it for you, please?"

"Oh, I don't think there's much point after all these years."

"Please just humor me. You have written it off anyway so it can't hurt you to let me try!"

Alberto handed the material over and shortly after that he left to get back to Marisa. Tia and Mavis and Claire sat there for a while longer so some further plotting and planning could occur. Once a rough plan was in place, Claire left with Mavis to get on with her responsibilities for the rest of her shift for the day at the co-op.

The next day, Tia was back at work but she managed to do some further research on the matter during her lunch break and that evening she called Claire.

"Claire, you will never guess what I found out!"

"*What?*"

"That B & T bank in Calgary did close down, just like Papa said, but all their important documents and the remaining occupied security boxes that nobody came forward to claim were moved to the founding branch right here in Edmonton."

"Wow!" Claire exclaimed.

"That was the good news. Now here comes the bad news. Accessing the strong boxes from the Calgary bank is not done in the regular way. They had to kind of squeeze them into one smallish vault here in Edmonton because of space constraints and, as a result, they couldn't re-implement the computerized double lock system. So as an extra safeguard they now require a higher level of identification. For papa to get into the box, which is in both his name and la Mamma's name, he has to show both birth certificates, his marriage certificate and both passports, but the passports don't have to be current. The person I spoke to said they understand that its mostly older people who don't necessarily travel any more who are holding those boxes and it would be unreasonable to expect them to all have a current passport."

"How generous of them!" Claire said dryly. "I'm assuming the identification issue won't present a problem for Alberto?"

"No, but I don't see how we can possibly get into Caroline's box, which was probably in her parents' names anyway."

"I think I may see a way," Claire said, and she got that scheming sound to her voice that always made Tia apprehensive when she heard it.

"Ugh," Tia groaned. "What are you going to do: create a diversion? Start a fire? Knock the guard over the head, open the boxes and run?"

"Something like that but hopefully not so dramatic," Claire said ruminatively.

She outlined her plan to Tia who objected at first but finally saw that it was the only way.

"When?" Tia asked in a resigned voice. "And this is assuming that papa will agree."

"Oh, I think I can get him to agree," Claire said quietly. And Tia knew she was right. Alberto would do just about anything for Claire in his effort to pay back what she had done for Marisa. He was convinced, and perhaps rightly so, that if it had not been for Claire's intervention when Marisa was in the hospital after her stroke, she would be dead now, murdered in her bed like the unfortunate others who had died during that terrible time.

"We need to do some research first, though," Claire said. "Did you find out the exact protocol for when a person wants to open a Calgary strongbox there?"

"Yes, the guard goes in with you—and they only allow in one person at a time—and he waits while you open the box, go through it and take out what you want."

"We're going to need two persons but I think I know how we can get around that," Claire said. "Unfortunately, the second person is going to have to be you, Tia."

Tia nodded, knowing it was the only way Claire's plan could work.

"Now, we need to find out what the traffic patterns are and when the most people are likely to be in the bank. And we need to know opening and closing hours and where the security cameras are. If they have one in the vault we need to know that in advance."

"When you say '*we*', I know you mean *me* because you would have no legitimate reason for talking to anyone there, but how do you suggest I find *that* out without giving the whole show away?" Tia asked.

"I don't know. I have to think on that a bit more," Claire said. "Oh! I just had one thought. Maybe I can phone and pretend to be a specialist in security cameras for banks and mention that we have a newly developed model that works particularly well in vaults because it has night vision so can see in the dark and also has a special wide angle lens and a build in sensor so if there is any movement in the vault it can sound an alarm. Then I'll just ask what their current system is and if all their vaults are covered. If the Calgary bank vault is as jammed with all the leftover security boxes, as you say it is, they might not have room for a camera. Then I'll just suggest that we would be willing to install one in there and can suspend it from the ceiling in a very small space. We would be willing to give them a three-month free trial if they'd consider switching over to our company after that, assuming they like the results. We would want to know if they might be interested in replacing all their vault cameras with our new model down the road. And I could offer to come out and show them the camera so they could see for themselves how it works. Of course, I would make the appointment for after our little intervention there, and, of course, I would have no intention of actually showing up! "

Tia just shuddered. "I never get over marveling at what a devious mind you have. I think that in a different life you could have been a master criminal and that thought is kind of scary!"

Claire just smirked unapologetically. "Tricky jobs call for tricky methods" was all she replied.

Tia sighed in resignation. "I'll try to find out the information you need tomorrow."

"And I'll get Matthew to set up a fake website and photo-shop some cameras in, angling them so they cannot be easily identified as belonging to other companies." Matthew was Amanda's grandson. He had specialized computer skills and had helped them with some of their investigations in the past. As a young teen he had been in trouble with the police for hacking into a closed computer system.

"God help us," was all Tia could think to say.

Chapter 12—The Rubber Hits the Road

It was a week later at 10 in the morning that Alberto parked his car around the corner from the B&T bank. He got out with Tia but Claire remained in the car, nervously fingering Alberto's spare set of keys. Just before they walked in the door together, Alberto adjusted himself to look older, frailer and less able than he was, as Tia had coached him.

Tia and Alberto noted the long line-up for the two bank clerks who were working and were grateful that they had been advised to go directly to the information desk. The assistant manager, Jan De Jong, arrived shortly to look after them. Meanwhile, Alberto was shuffling from one foot to another behind Tia, looking anxious and timid. After introductions and after stating why she would need to accompany her father, because of his limited knowledge of English, Jan directed them down a long hallway toward a room at the very back.

Jan unlocked the door to the vault, which was of course windowless, and he felt along the wall for the light switch to illuminate the pitch-black space. He closed the door securely behind them and silently pointed his finger along the lines of strong boxes stacked one on top of another until he reached number 247. He asked Tia to unlock the box with her key, which she did. Inside was a single sheet of paper that confirmed Alberto and Marisa to be the co-owners of 200 shares in the B & T, listing a security in the sum of $500.00 with the B & T bank, Branch # 2, Calgary, Alberta.

The paper was very straightforward and Tia made a show of sharing it with Alberto and explaining it to him in Italian. She was just wondering how long that could go on without it looking too suspicious when the light suddenly went out and the bank siren began blaring. They could hear the muffled sounds of people panicking in the outer part of the bank and suddenly they heard an even louder scream. "This woman is having a heart attack! Call an ambulance!"

Jan turned to them looking frazzled. "I have to help out there. Please leave now!" But Alberto suddenly stumbled and slumped against the wall. There were no chairs in the vault. Tia rushed to help him.

Tia turned to Jan who was looking increasingly anxious and torn, not able to fully discern his primary responsibility in such a chaotic situation. Tia reassured him. "Papa has these spells sometimes. He just needs to rest a minute. I will bring him out as soon as it is safe and I will close the door behind us when we leave. Don't worry!"

Jan took one quick glance around to reassure himself that no other boxes were open and then darted out of the room leaving the door open behind him. Tia quickly closed the door and turned off the light switch because she knew the emergency generator would be kicking in very soon. Then she darted a small penlight along the boxes below and to the right of their box because she had already observed that box 325 was located there. With fingers slippery with sweat, she fumbled as fast as she could to open the lock. Alberto pulled up his pant-leg and she stuffed the wad of papers she had found inside his sock and quickly relocked the box just as the door opened.

"Why are you still here with the door closed and why are you in the dark?" Jan demanded.

"The noise was making papa worse so I closed the door. He struggles with anxiety. Then I couldn't find the light switch to turn it on and I needed to be with him to calm him down."

"I thought I left it on,", Jan muttered. "In any case, is he alright to leave now? We have other issues to deal with and I need to handle them!"

"Yes, we're going!" Tia said sharply, her tone indicating that she didn't like the way they were being treated.

Jan hastened to explain. "I'm sorry if I seem curt but we really have some big issues to deal with!"

"I understand," Tia said softly. "I hope everything will be okay!" She grabbed her father's arm and guided him gently down the hall and out of the bank. They walked sedately together to the car and got in. Then they waited with the motor running.

About five minutes later, the back door opened and Claire hurled herself in and immediately crouched to the floor. "Go!" she said hoarsely, meanwhile ripping off a grey wig and a pair of old lady glasses.

Alberto put the turn signal on and pulled cautiously out into the street. Tia scanned the street behind them and the windows overlooking it to assure herself that Claire had not been observed. Satisfied, she signaled Albert to go and he drove to the corner and turned left, heading towards the branch of the public library closest to the bank. Meanwhile, Claire was on her phone and she remained on her phone giving directions to someone until they pulled up in an alley behind the library. Suddenly, the back door opposite where Claire was sitting opened and a tall man with grey hair, beard and moustache, a wrinkled, ruddy face and slouchy hat lumbered in. Again, Tia checked behind them to make sure they were not being observed and they then headed towards Wayne Gretzky Drive going south.

Matthew quickly removed the hair, wig and moustache and Claire stashed them in her large tote bag. Then she handed him a package of make-up remover pads, a plastic bag for discards and a mirror. He managed to remove most of the make-up and Claire did the rest. "Where are we going?" he asked in a weak voice and Claire could see that he was shaking.

"We're going to papa's house and I've called ahead to ask the assistant to take Marisa over to visit with Mavis. That way we won't risk being overheard. We should be there in about 20 minutes so just hang on, Matthew. I can see you're upset!"

Matthew looked down at his hands and saw that he was still wearing the thin, clear, close fitting latex gloves that Claire had given him. He ripped them off and tossed them in the discard bag with a shudder.

"It was bad, eh?" Claire asked sympathetically.

"I almost got caught! Do you realize what would have happened if I'd been caught? I would have lost *everything!* I would have been expelled from university and on top of that Amanda would have probably kicked me out in disgust and my parents would have given up on me entirely!"

"We would have been in pretty hot water ourselves!" Claire said matter-of-factly, but the point is we did *not* get caught and I'm pretty sure we're all in the clear now!"

Matthew just glared at her. "I am *never* doing anything like that again. *Don't even ask!"*

Tia turned to him soothingly. "We got what we were after and we couldn't have done it without you. If we ever manage to bring this killer to justice, it will only be because of you!" Matthew looked slightly mollified and Tia reached down and pulled the wad of papers out of her father's sock. "Here! I think after the terrible risk you took you deserve to be the first to see these. *You* go through them and tell us if there's anything useful there that will help direct us towards Caroline's killer!"

Matthew accepted them and it was clear that some of his old zest for puzzle solving was returning. He spent the next 10 minutes examining the papers without saying a word. The other people in the car remained silent, too, intuitively sensing that he needed this quiet time, both to concentrate and to calm down. Finally, Matthew spoke. "It looks like most of these papers are from her parents. There are several share certificates. Seems they invested quite a chunk of money in them, about $3000.00! Matthew had neatly divided the papers into two piles and now he turned to the second pile. "This pile is from more recent times according to some dates I found on them. And that matches with the hair and clothing styles in a couple of the pictures. The only other item is a copy of Caroline's will, dated two months ago. The lawyer's stamp is on it so it'll be easy enough to confirm."

"What does it say?" Claire asked curiously.

Matthew didn't answer immediately, obviously enjoying the opportunity for a little payback. Finally, when Tia also asked, he responded. Caroline left nothing to her cousin. She has designated Sylvia as executor and she's to be paid for the service of selling her home, disposing of her possessions and liquid assets as designated by a fee to measure 15% of the total net estate. Sylvia is also to see to it that her cat has a good home. The bulk of the estate is to be gifted to the SPCA. To her cousin, she leaves only a cameo that belonged to their grandmother and she gives directions as to where it is located."

"Wow!" Claire exclaimed. "We better get back there fast and kick that cousin out."

"There's one thing you're forgetting, Claire," Tia objected. "How are you going to explain having possession of the will? You hardly knew Caroline!"

"She *was* my trainer," Claire argued. "It *could* have happened."

"Can I see the will for a minute, please, Matthew?" Tia asked. Matthew immediately handed it over. Tia examined it carefully and then said, "There's no indication on it that this will was placed anywhere in particular. Therefore, she *could* have given it to Sylvia––and that is a far more likely scenario than pretending she gave it to *you*, Claire. From what you've told me, they were supposed to be quite close."

"Yes, I suppose you're right, Tia. Should I call her now?"

"We're almost home. You can call her then—but here's something else to think about. What we did today was clearly outside the law. The fewer people who know about it, the better, especially Matthew's part in it. We certainly have to keep *that* to ourselves!"

"But Sylvia was with me when we searched Caroline's place. *She's* the one who found the key! We have to tell her *something!*"

"Yes, and we need time to figure out what that something is. Hence, you better not call her now. We will go back to Alberto's house, debrief and work out a plan going forward."

"And celebrate!" Claire shouted. "Too bad we can't drink, eh, Tia?"

Chapter 13: One Puzzle Leads to Another

The four of them settled down in Alberto's empty house to go over the events of the morning. "Matthew, you go first," Claire directed.

"I had no problem accessing the library computers. Nobody else was using them at that time of the morning and I was able to grab the newest one that had more memory and speed than the others. I had already experimented at home with getting in the back door of the security system guarding the town's power supply and determining where the bank was on the grid. I just kept my finger on the button and when I got your text, Claire, I sent the order.

"That was the easy part! But when you texted 'done', Claire, I then needed to pull up the code and delete it so there would be no traces left on the library computer. It took a couple of minutes to do that, and that's when the security guard came along! I managed to close the screen but I'm not sure if he had a glimpse of the code being deleted or not, and he seemed very suspicious.

"'You've been on that computer a long time' he commented. 'We usually ask people to limit their use to half an hour.'

"'I'm sorry, sir' I said, in as croaky a voice as I could manage. 'I'm just trying to help my grand-daughter. She's in a spot of bother, if you know what I mean.' Then I looked around and mentioned to him that there were a number of the guest computers not in use. 'Do you think I could just keep helping her a while longer? I promise if somebody comes along and needs the computer I'll give it up. But she really needs my help. She has nobody else to turn to!'"

"*That* was clever!" Alberto interjected.

"*I* thought so when I made it up!" Claire could not help saying. Tia smirked and thought to herself, *Claire does have her ego!*

"Anyway," Matthew went on, focused on his story, the guard agreed and walked away. The trouble is that there were a couple of other users there by then and they heard what I said. Then they proceeded to gawk at my computer to see if they could read the supposed exchange between my 'grand-daughter' and me."

"What did you *do*?" Tia asked

"I stood up and tried to block the computer while looking feeble and upset at the same time. It was terrible! I finally got the code all deleted but I'm just not sure that somebody didn't see what I was doing!"

"As long as they didn't see you getting into the car!" Claire said.

"I was watching the whole time and I kept watching until we pulled away," Tia said. "I didn't see anyone."

"Let's just hope!" Alberto muttered. "All they would need to do is get the license number. They could have done that without even being noticed."

"I *did* smear some mud on it this morning," Claire said.

Tia snickered. "Oh, you are *bad!*" Alberto grinned.

Matthew looked more relaxed at this point and Tia quickly related their adventures. Then Claire sketched out the drama of her false heart attack—in a little more detail than was strictly necessary, Tia thought. When she finished and had been suitably lauded for her acting abilities, Claire said, "Okay, we better discuss our next steps," and she shared her thoughts on possible directions.

"It seems to me our priority right now is to let Sylvia know about the contents of Caroline's will so she can oust the cousin from the house before things start disappearing, assuming that isn't happening already! This is what I suggest we tell her. We managed to get into Caroline's family strong box and empty it and she is *not* to know how or to share that information with anybody else—*ever!* There's a new will and to enforce it she will first have to explain how she came by it. The easiest thing is to say that Caroline gave it to her with papers for safekeeping because she was feeling threatened. Since Sylvia was named as the executor this makes sense."

"McCoy already interviewed her about Caroline. How is she going to explain not mentioning that?" Tia objected.

"She can say he was asking her about the murder investigation and she didn't think it was relevant."

"Pretty thin!" Tia warned. "I don't think he's going to buy it! Also, there's the little matter of the suspicious break-in last week. He might think it very convenient that this will has suddenly materialized."

"He can think what he likes. It's what he can prove that counts! Anyway, I think the first thing to do is to contact Sylvia. Secondly, she should get in touch with the lawyer who wrote it up as soon as possible. And thirdly, she needs to meet up with the cousin and show her the will."

"Why don't you just call her?" Matthew suggested, "instead of making all these plans for her while she's still in the dark!"

They all agreed and Claire made the call. Sylvia was predictably stunned. "Caroline never said a word to me!" But once she had recovered enough to properly absorb the news, she took charge of the situation. "I'll call the lawyer right now and arrange to see him. I'll also call Caroline's cousin and ask her if she'd like to come with me. That seems the best way of dealing with the issue—through a third party."

"How are you going to contact the cousin?"

"I'll phone the front desk and ask to be put through to Caroline's apartment on the house phone. But before I do all that, I'll come over now and pick up the will and the other papers if that's okay with you."

"Uh, okay, Sylvia. But just give me a few minutes first. I'm busy doing something else right now."

"It'll take me 20 minutes to get there. Is that good enough?"

"Yes, that should work. See you then, Sylvia. I'll be at the co-op." Claire hung up the phone, grabbed the papers and quick walked across the street to the co-op so she could access the photocopier. She wasn't satisfied that she had gleaned all the information that might be relevant from them and wanted her own copy but Sylvia didn't need to know that!"

Later that evening, Sylvia called to let Claire know what had happened at the lawyer's office. "He told me and Caroline's cousin, Vanessa, that Caroline came in about seven weeks ago to discuss making a will and they had worked out the details at that time. Two weeks later, she came back to sign it. She took one copy with her and he filed the other one in his office. He showed Vanessa his own copy and she carefully compared the two documents. She could not find anything to dispute, although she's still finding it hard to believe that all Caroline left her was the ring. However, she agreed to take it and go.

The lawyer also gave me a key to Caroline's apartment that she had left with him to pass on to me if something happened to her. I gave it to the cousin. She's leaving tomorrow morning since there doesn't seem to be any reason for her to remain in Edmonton longer and she wants to get back to work. She told me she'd lock up when she goes and leave the key with the desk clerk at the front desk, with instructions to give it back to me. She, of course, doesn't know that I already have one! I did feel a bit badly for her and asked her if she'd like to look through Caroline's clothes to see if there was anything there she'd like but she wasn't interested. Valerie is quite a big girl and nothing Caroline had would fit her anyway.

"Wait a minute!" Claire said, alarmed. "She can't just leave like that! She thought she was the heir so that makes her an obvious suspect. McCoy will definitely want to talk to her!"

"You're right, Claire. You better call him."

"I'm on it. I'll call you back when I find out what he plans," and she hung up the phone.

Inspector McCoy was decidedly cool on the phone but he did appreciate the information. Sylvia had obtained Vanessa's cell number and passed it on to Claire so she was able to give it to the inspector. After writing it down, he hung up immediately so he could call her. Of course, Claire heard nothing back but then she was not expecting to. Even when McCoy was on more friendly terms with her he wasn't much for sharing. *It doesn't matter anyway,* she told herself. *I doubt that Vanessa is the killer, but then who is?*

Claire spent the evening at home going over and over the papers she had photocopied. She also studied the pictures carefully. She had given copies to Sylvia, reasoning that she wouldn't know the difference anyway—and Claire wanted to peruse every last detail of the originals. There were three pictures: two of couples and one of two men. The latter was clearly unusual. It looked like the bigger man was threatening the smaller one with a knife! In one of the couples photographs, the pair were clearly at a bar drinking.

The woman's glass had a slice of lime in it and looked like it might be a gin and tonic. It also looked like she was at least six month's pregnant. The man was nursing a beer and looking at her in what appeared to be a judgmental manner. The third picture was of the same couple but they looked a few years younger in it. The man was holding a document that looked like a deed to something and he was regarding it gleefully.

Too bad I can't see it more clearly, Claire muttered to herself. *If it was on the computer I could enlarge it and play with the contrast and maybe bring out some more detail. Well, I'll just have to go old school.* Claire searched out a large magnifying glass and adjusted the desk lamp for maximum illumination. Then she studied the photo carefully. There was a smudge on the title line that appeared to be a name but, no matter how she adjusted the magnifier, Claire couldn't make it out. She threw the picture down in frustration, flipping it over in the process. And that's when she noticed the letter *C* lightly penciled on the back corner.

Claire stared at the C, thinking. Then she quickly flipped over the other two pictures. There was an A on one and a B on the other!

Chapter 14: More Complications

The next day passed uneventfully and Claire kept busy at work. Bill was home with a cold and she had to cancel the trip to the science center she had planned with Roscoe so she could look after him. She finally gave up searching for an activity they could both enjoy since their needs were quite different and in the afternoon she put on an action movie with Bruce Willis in it that they could all enjoy.

That night, Claire had trouble sleeping. In the morning, she woke up from a scary dream and said to herself, *This whole mess is beyond what I can deal with. And this warm/cold situation with McCoy is also getting too difficult to cope with. Something has to be done!* As always when she was stressed and feeling out of her depth, Claire fell back on her stock of adages and platitudes. The one that came to mind now was, "How to kill two birds with one stone!"

Claire phoned Sylvia who hadn't yet left for work as it was barely 7 a.m. She sounded sleepy and also surprised to be receiving such an early phone call. Lack of impulse control was one of Claire's ongoing issues. Once she decided on a course of action she seemed absolutely incapable of waiting to an appropriate moment or time to share it.

"It's Claire, Sylvia. I need to ask you to do ..."

"Oh, Claire!" Sylvia stopped for a long yawn and Claire belatedly checked the time. "I was going to call you. I already called the police last night."

"What happened?" Claire demanded anxiously.

"There was a break-in to Caroline's apartment yesterday afternoon. The place was ransacked!"

"Do you think your cousin did it before she left?"

"No, I drove her to the airport yesterday. She couldn't get the morning flight she'd wanted but she got the 2 p.m. flight and after I dropped her off I returned to the apartment on purpose just to check it out. Everything looked fine then and nothing seemed to be missing. Anyway, last night around eight, I decided to go back to the apartment. Caroline had a couple of nice plants that needed watering and I thought I might as well just take them home so I didn't have to bother going back and forth there all the time. But when I went in, everything was in total chaos and both plants had been dropped to the floor and smashed and the soil was spread all around. It was as if the intruder was looking for something he thought might have been buried in one of them!"

"What other damage was there?"

"No real damage. It didn't look like vandalism. Just a big mess! All the drawers were pulled out and the stuff scattered all over. The bedding was off the bed and the mattress had been thrown off as if the intruder was checking underneath for something. All the boxes in the closet had been rifled through."

"What did McCoy say?"

"Well, he's still suspicious about the last break-in so you can expect a call from him."

"Oh, for Pete's sake! As if I'd ever be capable of ransacking somebody's house. That man is impossible!" Claire exploded.

"Well, that's the situation anyway," Sylvia said. After a pause she added, "But you said you had something to talk to me about?"

"Yes. Before I gave them to you, I looked through the papers and pictures that Tia and Alberto got from the bank and they raise questions we don't have the resources to answer. You're going to have to pass them on to McCoy and in order to do so you're going to have to explain how they legitimately came into your possession. I'm thinking that the best thing to do is to simply tell him that Caroline gave them to you for safekeeping. If he asks why, you can say that she was scared of somebody but didn't give you any more information. How does that sound?"

"I don't know how that would work because he'll just ask why I didn't tell him before when he interviewed me about her murder!"

"You can say it was a private matter between you and her and had nothing to do with the murder."

"And the supposed threat?"

"Okay, let's say she was cleaning up and came across this cache of papers from her parents. She didn't know if they were important or not and asked you to go through them because she found it too depressing— after losing them so suddenly in that car accident. If you found anything important she needed to deal with, you could tell her. Otherwise, she was just going to put them away again until she felt ready to deal with them. Oh—and this happened just a couple of days before she was killed so you never had a chance to go through them or get back to her."

"And how does that fit with your blackmail theory— which is the whole point of passing them on to your inspector? Caroline would hardly pass on her blackmail evidence to me!"

"Ugh!" Claire responded. "I forgot about that! "Okay, here's another way. It *would* have made sense for Caroline to give you a copy of the will in advance. In fact, I don't know why she didn't."

"Maybe she wasn't completely sure that she wanted me to be the executrix and decided to think on it a bit more."

"I guess that's possible. From what I understand, you really weren't all that close to her. You've only known her a couple of years, right?"

"Yes, only since she came to work here at the gym."

"So the question is why didn't she want somebody she'd known longer to be the executor?"

"Maybe she was thinking that if something *did* happen to her there were papers in her possession from her past life that she didn't want these others to see but me, being a relatively new person in her life, wouldn't grasp the significance of them?"

"Yes! *That* should work! But just to cement the idea in McCoy's mind, you can mention that Caroline always seemed to be on the secretive side, as if she was hiding something!"

"Fine, but how would I have found those papers and pictures in the first place?" Remember, the police thoroughly searched her place before I even had a chance to go there."

"As the executor it's up to you to dispose of her stuff as part of settling her estate. And now it's also up to you to clean up the mess. So you just say you went back there and were putting things back in the boxes and came across these papers and pictures right at the bottom of one of them." And after a pause, she added. "As for the police going through the stuff, that just helps to support the basic point. They could have seen the pictures and not considered them important because they didn't know what they were looking for! But now that the place has been so thoroughly searched it just suggests that somebody is very anxious to get something back that Caroline had! And a likely reason for that is blackmail."

"Okay, I'll give it a try—but how will I explain taking the pictures and letters from Caroline's house in the first place?"

"They looked suspicious to you because there was no logical reason for them to be stored away together unless there was a connection between the two!"

"Yes…. That does make sense. Okay, I'll *do* it! Wish me luck!"

That afternoon, after Claire finished her shift at the co-op, she met up with Sylvia again at the Starbucks near the gym. Sylvia informed her that she'd passed the papers onto Inspector McCoy. He was interested but disappointed that there were only photocopies of the pictures because they weren't clear enough to make identification possible.

Claire winced when she heard this but said nothing. After a pause, she finally admitted, "*I* kept the pictures and gave you photocopies. I wanted to study them further because I just had a funny feeling there was a clue there."

Sylvia looked at her but said nothing. Claire knew she was being silently judged and went on hastily to justify herself. "Look! This business of uncovering murderers is very difficult work. You can't win unless you use every trick at your disposal. That's why private eyes have a reputation for being sneaky—and seedy."

"What does the seedy part have to do with it?"

"Well, I guess you can get so obsessed with doing this job that you forget about everything including personal hygiene. *I* can't afford to get that wrapped up because I still have to function in the real world, not just the under-world."

"Oh, I see," Sylvia said, although she didn't. She was beginning to understand why Tia talked about Claire having a convoluted brain.

The next day Sylvia called Inspector McCoy and informed him that she had done some more rooting around at Caroline's apartment and had come across the original pictures. She also mentioned, as per Claire's coaching, that she had found some letters on the back of the pictures and she was wondering if they matched up with the letters she'd observed on the tops of the ones she'd given to him.

"I'll send someone over right now to pick them up and I'll definitely check into that. It may be a useful clue!" Then in an uncharacteristic move away from his usual professionalism, he gave her a compliment. "It's so nice to work with someone who can track down information, but then has the good sense to pass it on to me instead of mucking around in the situation herself!"

When Sylvia later shared this conversation, Claire knew immediately who he was talking about and felt momentarily depressed. Clearly she still had a lot of ground to make up in her relationship with McCoy. However, she perked up the next day after hearing that McCoy had phoned Sylvia back. With a considerateness he'd never shown to Claire, the inspector informed Sylvia that after putting the pictures through their facial recognition system, he'd been able to get a hit on one of the single males. He was serving a seven-year term for manslaughter in Lansing, Michigan, and Caroline had been the star witness at his trial.

Chapter 15: Radio Silence and Other Priorities

Later that evening, Sylvia, Claire and Tia were sitting around a table at a Moxie's Restaurant near Sylvia's apartment where they had agreed to meet. "Well, what's this 'frightening news' that McCoy shared with you?" Claire asked. The slightly jealous note in her voice was barely perceptible but Tia caught it.

Sylvia told them then and they both sat there silently. "Well?" she finally asked.

"Where exactly did Caroline witness this murder; did McCoy say?" Tia asked.

"Detroit."

"What was she doing there?" Claire asked.

"It happened before I knew her or knew her well and she never discussed it with me," Sylvia replied. Tia and Claire both looked disappointed. "Bu-t," Sylvia went on, clearly relishing her chance to look like a real detective, "I phoned her cousin and *she* told me. Apparently, Caroline attended a three-day fitness workshop there three years ago to learn about a new training approach and some specialized exercises that had been recently developed to increase core strength."

"And there was a murder at the workshop?" Tia asked, shocked.

"No. What happened was this. Caroline didn't know anybody there and she was bored on the last evening because there were no special events planned so she went for a walk through a park near her hotel.

"And?"

"She had just turned around and was walking back when she noticed two men around the corner on the other side of the street. They appeared to be arguing and as she got closer she saw that one of them had a knife. She took that picture just as he raised the knife to strike the other man. Then she called 911. As it happened there were a couple of beat cops nearby and they responded to the general call that was sent out. They arrived just after the other man was killed and the first man was still standing there. He ran when he saw them but they caught up with him and handcuffed him. Caroline told them that she'd seen the whole thing and she had to go in and give her statement and then she had to come back and testify when the trial came up. Her testimony and the picture she took were enough to convict him and he got seven years for manslaughter."

"Wow! But if he's in jail then he could not have been the one who ransacked her apartment," Claire pointed out.

"But that's just it!" Sylvia said dramatically, having saved the best for last. "He escaped from prison 27 days ago and the police have no idea where he is."

"Well, if he crossed the border into Canada the border guards would know about it. The American police always notify them when somebody is on the loose," Tia said.

"Inspector McCoy already checked. There's been no sign of him."

"But he could have crossed illegally," Claire argued. "Lots of people do these days as we all know."

"But why would he come here? To get a picture that had already been used in evidence against him? That doesn't make any sense."

"Wait!" Claire said excitedly. "Twenty-seven days ago Caroline was still alive. Maybe he's the one who killed her!"

"But then what reason would he have to come to Caroline's apartment?" Tia asked. "She was killed at the gym."

Claire sighed. "It doesn't look like he could have trashed the apartment and it doesn't seem possible that Vanessa did it so who does that leave? It seems to me that we're at a dead end."

Sylvia looked at the depressed faces of her friends and finally opened her mouth to speak. "I didn't want to say anything out of loyalty to Caroline but I've been going through her stuff since I'm now legally responsible for dealing with it. I've run across a number of personal items and pieces of clothing that clearly belong to a man or men. All the clothes seem to match in size, however, so they could belong to one man."

"What size and what all did you find?" Claire asked eagerly, her former malaise now forgotten.

"They're a medium size but in tall lengths so maybe somebody on the tall side but thin or fine boned. I found two sweat shirts, a jacket and a pair of jeans. None of them are small enough to have fit Caroline."

"So she did have a new boyfriend!" Claire mused. It doesn't sound like those clothes would fit the ex. He's definitely on the bulky side and not all that tall. I wonder ... I think I know how we might get a description of him!"

"How?" Tia asked.

"That snoop next door! If she was spying out her window at 11 o'clock at night when she saw *us*, the chances are that she cracked her door open to peak out every time she heard the elevator ding. She might have seen him!"

"Well, what are you waiting for? Go ask her," Tia ordered.

"I can't—and neither can Sylvia. She might recognize us. Would you...?"

But Tia was already shaking her head. "What possible excuse could I use for asking her anything about Caroline?"

"I guess you're right," Claire said. She turned to Sylvia. "You're going to have to phone McCoy and tell him what you found. Since he now knows that you're the executor that shouldn't be a problem. You'll also have to remind him, very casually, that he received information from the neighbor once before and maybe she'd also noticed this man when he came to visit Caroline."

"I guess I can do that," Sylvia agreed. But inside Claire was fuming. This was exactly the sort of thing she liked to do herself and she was very frustrated that she couldn't approach the neighbor directly. Tia looked at her with amusement, guessing just what was going through Claire's mind. "You'll have to trust that McCoy knows what he's doing, Claire. He's a policeman, after all!"

Claire blushed at having her thoughts read so clearly but nodded her head in agreement. "Well, where do we go from here?" she asked, partly to get past the awkward moment. "Sylvia, have you followed up on that maintenance man yet?"

"Yes. I had an early morning client yesterday and he was there when I arrived and still working when I finished the session with my client. So I nipped over to Starbucks and bought him a latte with extra espresso in it. That's how he likes it. He was very happy to have it and in a talkative mood. Apparently, he was there most of the night. Something had gone seriously wrong with the heating system but he finally got it working properly again. After, we talked for a bit. I mentioned Caroline's murder."

"Did you find out if he'd been doing any work at the gym that week?" Claire asked.

"I did—and he immediately got defensive. He said the police had already talked to him but, like he told them, he wasn't even in town the week she was killed. He was at a heating workshop in Spokane, Washington. It was on techniques for trouble shooting and fixing the new, high efficiency furnaces. And he hung around the rest of the week visiting his older sister who lives there. She could vouch for him being there and so could his son—for when he left."

"What son? Where does *he* live?"

"Ronald. Ronald, he calls him. He's 23 and he's been living with his dad for the past six months, helping him sometimes with his work. Stan said that he and his wife split up when Ronald was eleven and he lived with her until his mother remarried this past year. Apparently, Ronald doesn't feel too welcome there anymore."

"What kind of work has he been doing?"

"Stan was kind of vague about that but I get the impression not much of anything. The only thing Stan talked about was how much his son was into body building."

"Didn't you tell me once that Caroline was into body building? Maybe they knew each other."

"If they did, I think Stan would have mentioned it."

"Not if he was protecting his son," Tia pointed out.

"That's true, I suppose," Sylvia agreed.

"Okay, this is something that has to be checked out and this time *I'm* going to contact McCoy!" Claire stated firmly.

"And say what?" Sylvia asked. "*I'm* the one who talked to Stan about his son. Don't you think it makes more sense for me to call Inspector McCoy? How are you going to explain even knowing about him?"

"I'll just say I overheard someone at the gym talking about him."

"That someone would have to be me since I'm pretty well the only one who ever talks to Stan now that Caroline is gone. We were the only two who came in early enough to see him."

"*Fine,* but does McCoy know that? I don't *think* so!" Claire said smugly.

Sylvia sniffed. "I'm not a gossip and I don't want anyone thinking I *am* a gossip. Besides, Inspector McCoy asked me to keep my ears open and report to him anything I heard. He told me that he felt confident he could trust my discretion and I wouldn't do something foolish and get into trouble like some people he could mention!"

Claire gritted her teeth when she heard this. She knew exactly who McCoy had been referring to—and she decided that she really didn't like Sylvia very much.

Tia silently took all this in and smothered a smile. "I'm calling him!" she said. This maintenance person has to come in sometimes during the day and presumably his otherwise idle son has accompanied him sometimes. Therefore, other people working here besides you may well have been aware of him."

Tia stood up at that moment and said, "Claire and I have to leave now. We have another meeting we need to be at."

Claire raised her eyebrows but said nothing and allowed herself to be led out by Tia. She realized, as had Tia, that she'd been very close to saying something she would regret.

Chapter 16: Claire Redeems Herself

"McCoy here," was all Claire heard when he answered the phone, even though Claire knew that he would've recognized her number.

"Hello, it's Claire," she said coolly. "I have some information for you."

"What?" he asked tersely.

"It's about Stan Polansky's 23-year old son. Did you know he's been living with Stan for the past six months and that he's unemployed but helps Stan out with his work from time to time?"

"Stan was away when the murder happened. We've confirmed his alibi."

"Sure, but did he have his keys with him—and did his son, Ronald, know the security code at the gym?"

"I'll check on that," McCoy replied. "Thanks for the information. I've got to go." And he hung up the phone.

Claire sat holding the dead phone in her hand listening to the dial tone for a minute. Then she realized that she'd forgotten about the body building connection. She phoned him back.

"What?" he said impatiently when he picked up the phone, thereby confirming that he did indeed recognize her number.

"He was into body building. You might ask him about that—and ask him if he ever ran into Caroline while training or at body building contests. I understand that Caroline was into bodybuilding as well, and she even won prizes a couple of times. You might check with the gyms that have trainers specialized in that area while you're at it to see if either one was known there. There are only a couple of those in the city." And with that, Claire hung up the phone without waiting for a response. Two could play the same game!

Claire was in her fifth month of pregnancy at this point. The ultrasound had indicated that she'd been further along than either she or the doctor had realized. Tia, on the other hand was only midway through her third month. As the days passed, Claire was increasingly preoccupied with finding a replacement and she decided that she really must talk to Tia to see if she had any suggestions. As usual, Tia was very busy at work but agreed to meet Claire for lunch in their staff cafeteria.

When Claire arrived at the cafeteria, she was annoyed to see that Hazel was sitting with Tia. Hazel was one of the cleaning staff at the hospital where Tia worked and she had assisted Tia and Claire in flushing out a killer who had been terrorizing it when Tia's mother was there. Ordinarily, Claire would be happy to see her but right now all she could think about was that she needed Tia to herself and that surely was not too much to ask for the crummy half hour that was all Tia could give her.

"Hi, Claire!" Hazel said brightly. "Great to see you again. Congratulations on your pregnancy! You must be excited!"

"Hi, yourself—and the same—and yes," Claire replied but with somewhat less enthusiasm. She looked at Tia.

Tia just looked back at her and said, "I'm pretty sure I know why you're so anxious to see me today, Claire, and I'm way ahead of you. Why don't you ask Hazel what she's been doing lately?"

Claire frowned in response but turned to Hazel and dutifully asked, "What's happening with you these days?"

"Well, for one thing, my mother remarried a really nice man, an electrician. They moved to a better place and he's doing great with my younger brothers and sister! My mother doesn't need my help anymore so I moved too and got my own place. It isn't much because I'm still saving all I can for school but I'm really happy to have my own space."

"Wow, that must be quite a change! And when do you think you can start your nursing program? Have you been taking any part-time courses?"

"Well, that's a funny story."

"What do you mean?"

"You remember the night you had to rush me to the hospital because of anaphylactic shock?"

"*Oh,* yeah! How could I forget it?"

"Well, something happened that night—but I didn't really work it out until a few months later. What I finally realized was that I'd had a romantic view of hospital life and now that I had experienced the real thing, I knew that it really wasn't where I wanted to spend my working years."

"Oh? I'm kind of sorry to hear that. You were so keen at one point. So are you planning to keep on with your cleaning job here at the hospital?"

"Temporarily, yes, but I've already moved to part-time. I've been taking courses to become an educational assistant. I decided that I want to work with people, not people's bodies."

"I thought you didn't care for children that much? You told me once that you'd had more than enough of kids because you had to help out so much with your brothers and sister."

"You're right about that!" Hazel replied, grimacing. "I would far rather work with adults. You remember you gave me the chance to work in your co-op setting for a few months? I really enjoyed that—but I haven't found any courses that would prepare me for that kind of work."

"That's true. The field is really underdeveloped. However, a lot of work is being done to professionalize it and there are courses available, an entire course that you can take on-line exploring every aspect relevant to working with adults with developmental disabilities. There are also various one or two day workshops available on everything from medication administration to understanding the abuse protocol to CPR and First Aid."

"Oh!" Hazel said in surprise. "I didn't know that! Can you give me the contact information?"

"Definitely. But there's something else you should know. The people who work best in this field do so not because of any particular qualifications. They need a good heart and a good attitude and good boundaries."

"What does that mean?"

"It means they have to be genuinely interested in and caring about other people, whatever problems or limitations they may have. But they also have to care about and look after themselves and not get carried away trying to save the world. At the same time, they need to be able to park their own problems at home when they're at work and if they don't like something that's happening at work, they need to be able to try to fix it up front, not gossip about it behind the administrator's back. And for that they need to be able to be assertive and directive when necessary, not scared of authority and at the same time resentful of it!"

"Wow, I get that! We have some of those same issues around here; right, Tia?"

"Well, not so much any more."

"Yeah, and that's because of you."

"It's because of all of us, agreeing to work together and to try to make things better!"

At that point Claire gave a large sigh.

Hazel, always sensitive to other people's needs, was quick to ask, "What's wrong, Claire?"

Claire looked at her and hesitated for a moment. "Well that's why I wanted to talk to Tia today. Something is very wrong. I'm five months pregnant and I have no idea who I can get to take my place at the co-op. It's been working very well but it's always a delicate balancing act. It could fall apart very easily and that's what I'm worried about. In fact, I can hardly sleep at night for thinking about it."

"What about the staff you have now? Can't any of them step up and take your place?"

"No, not that I can see. It needs to be somebody who sees this as a career, not as a stopgap measure before moving on to something else. Most of my employees are students who work part-time, and they're looking forward to professional careers in areas like physiotherapy or nursing or education."

"But you do have some full-time people," Tia pointed out.

"Yes, but they happen to all be immigrants with a limited command of English and of the way our system works. They wouldn't be able to handle all the paperwork nor do they feel sufficiently confident in themselves that they could handle the rest of the staff with the necessary degree of authority."

"I wish I could do it," Hazel said. "I'd just love to do a job like that—but I don't have the qualifications or even the experience."

Claire looked at her and said softly, "I desperately want to find somebody who'd just love to do my job, for all the right reasons. And I only have four months to train them and bring them up to speed." She looked at Hazel hopefully.

Tia interrupted at that point. "I think it could work—and that's why I asked Hazel to join us today. I've worked with her for going on two years now and I can speak very positively to her work ethic and her capacity to interact effectively with other people. Do you have any staff openings right now, Claire?"

"As a matter of fact, I have to fill two afternoon/overnight shifts. The same person has been handling that position very competently for the past three years but now her husband got a good job in a small town north of Edmonton and they're moving. This Thursday will be her last day."

Hazel looked meaningfully at Tia. "Hazel's scheduled to work here Thursday but I can get a substitute. She can go to the co-op and try things out with your assistant. That will give you both a better idea of whether or not there's any point going forward with this idea that none of us right now has the courage to even say out loud!"

Claire nodded her head in agreement. But Tia noticed that her eyes were shiny with unshed tears. Claire got up to leave though her sandwich remained on the plate before her untouched. "I'll see you Thursday at four, then, Hazel," she said, and exited quickly.

Hazel looked at Tia. "Just go there Thursday," Tia said. And don't talk about what you don't know, especially to the person training you. Just focus on learning all you can and connecting with the clients. Then phone me when you get home. I have faith!"

Chapter 17: The Twists and Turns of Life

It was 10:20 at night when the phone rang. Tia had left it on the bathroom counter and fumbled to reach it. "Hello," she said faintly.

"Tia? Tia?"

"Yes."

"It's me, Hazel. It was great!"

Hazel, help me please! Jimmy's not here."

"What?"

"Call Claire. I need her. Right *now!*"

Claire arrived exactly 12 minutes later, half dressed and having seriously broken the speed record on the way over. She twisted her emergency key to Tia's house in the lock, hurled the door open and raced down the hallway. The bathroom light was on but everywhere else was dark and silent. Claire threw the door open to find Tia lying on the floor and bleeding profusely. *Miscarriage!* Claire guessed, and grabbed a heavy coat from the closet to drape around Tia's shivering body. Then she called 911 and headed for Mario's room. Tia's 12-year-old son was sleeping soundly and she shook him gently by the shoulder.

"Aunty Claire! What's wrong?"

"Is your father really away?"

"Yes. He's on an emergency job in Wetaskiwin. He probably won't be back for a couple of days."

"Mario, listen to me. Run next door and see if Amanda can come over. She's not answering her phone. I think she turns it off at night."

"Why?" he asked fearfully.

"Your mother is sick and the ambulance is coming. I have to go with her. If Amanda can't come you need to stay here with your sister and look after her if necessary. Can you do that?"

"Yes, but mamma! I want to see mamma!" He started to cry.

"Just go. *I'm* looking after your mamma. Just go quickly. I hear the ambulance and I can't leave if you aren't here."

Mario pulled on his slippers and rushed out the door. He returned just as Tia was being loaded into the ambulance and ran to her. "Don't worry, mamma. Don't worry about us. Amanda is coming as soon as she can and I'll be here with Marion. Just get better, please." And he started to cry.

Claire grabbed him and hugged him furiously. "Don't worry. She'll be okay. Just go to Marion. Be strong!" She jumped in the ambulance and with that they were off.

When they reached the emergency entrance at the hospital, Tia was wheeled straight into the delivery room. Claire huddled in a chair in the waiting room trying over and over to reach Jimmy on the phone with no results. Finally, she called the emergency number for the electrical company for which he worked. She explained the situation to the on-call person who promised to do her best to get a message to him. Then she called Mario to let him know what was happening.

"If you were here, you'd be sitting in the waiting room just like me, Mario. There's nothing more we can do for her right now. I will phone you just as soon as I hear anything—and I have an emergency call into your father." She could hear Mario sobbing on the phone and then Amanda picked it up. Claire explained all over what was happening and Amanda assured her that she would be there and the children would be okay. Claire hung up then. There was nothing more she could do.

Oh! she thought to herself, *I better call Dan. He'll be worried about me, and wondering what's happening.* She made the call and had just managed to give Dan the bare facts when the surgeon emerged and she had to hang up the phone.

"Is Mrs. Elves' husband here?" he asked. Claire had had the presence of mind to grab Tia's purse.

"No, he's working out of town and I haven't been able to reach him yet—but just then her phone rang. She glanced at it and saw that it was Jimmy. Claire handed it directly to the surgeon and said, "This is him."

"The surgeon took the phone and once Jimmy had identified himself he told him the situation. "Your wife has had a miscarriage and it looks like she's been having the same problem as in her previous pregnancy when her blood pressure rose so high. I think she'll be okay but she's lost a lot of blood. Do we have your permission to give her a transfusion?" A nurse had come to stand by his side and Jimmy's response must have been positive because the nurse turned on her heel and sped away to organize the transfusion. The surgeon then went on talking to Jimmy. "Yes, I believe she'll be okay but it's just lucky she arrived when she did. She wouldn't have lasted much longer." On hearing this, Claire finally broke down but suddenly she felt strong arms around her and a coat was gently thrown over her shoulders.

"Dan!" Claire gasped. "What are you doing here? Who's with Jessie?"

"You're not the only one who can call on a neighbor in the middle of the night!"

At that point, the surgeon handed the phone back to Claire. "The husband has asked that you be allowed to see her so follow me please."

"Jimmy," Claire said into the phone. "I'm on my way in to see her. Hang on. If she can talk I'll give her the phone." Dan trailed behind them, not knowing what else to do.

Tia lay in a narrow gurney in the recovery room looking as white as the sheets that encased her. She was barely conscious but Claire laid the phone gently by her ear after turning the speaker on. "Tia! Are you there?" Jimmy's voice echoed hollowly through the phone.

"Ji –Jimmy," Tia stuttered. Claire grabbed her hand. "I'm here, too, Tia."

She felt Tia grip her hand faintly and then the surgeon said, "Okay, that's enough. You'll have to leave now. I'm going to give her a strong sedative and she'll be asleep soon. I suggest you come back in the morning.

Dan and Claire walked out of the room with Jimmy still on the phone. "Claire, how does she look? How bad is it? *Tell* me!" he pleaded.

"I think, like the surgeon said, that she's going to be okay. She just needs to rest and recover," Claire said.

"Well, I guess you won't have to worry about getting those baby supplies now," he said harshly. But Claire forgave him for she knew how upset he was.

Chapter 18: Another Unexpected Event

Two weeks had passed and Tia had slowly recovered. Claire had seen little of her, just one short visit for which Dan had driven her. She had contracted a severe cold after rushing out that night to take care of Tia without dressing properly for the weather. Although Dan was usually quite laid back and tolerant of Claire's activities, this had brought out another side of him. He had cancelled a couple of previously scheduled meetings and stayed home with Claire for an entire week to look after her and ensure that she remained in bed and rested. "We don't want another miscarriage," was all he would say grimly when she objected.

During their brief visit to Tia, Dan had talked with Jimmy while Claire and Tia had their own private get-together in the bedroom. Claire could see that her friend was well on the way to recovering physically but not so much psychologically. Finally, Claire broached the elephant in the room. "Are you going to try again?"

"I don't know. I'd like to but Jimmy is dead against it. Unless I can bring him around there's no hope. I'm not going to trick him into it."

"Do you think he has a point?"

"Of course. We both met with the doctor. He explained how dangerous it would be with this blood pressure thing that happens. It's just...."

"Okay, Tia. I understand—but I'm scared, too, of you getting pregnant again. The doctor said at the time that you almost died. It was touch and go. And you had the same problem when Marion was born. I don't think you'll be so lucky a third time."

"I know," Tia said, a note of resignation in her voice. "I need to be here to raise my children and to look after Jimmy."

"And for *yourself!*" Claire added, her voice rising. "Don't you think it's time you thought of that—after all you've been through in your life?"

Tia just looked at her. "And there's the job. I really love my job, you know."

"You loved it well enough to go back to work when Marion was just a couple of months old. And, as I recall, everyone, including Marion, was better off for it because of how much it improved your mood!"

Tia just sighed and soon after that the visit ended. Claire had a doctor's appointment later that afternoon.

Claire was in her seventh month of pregnancy at this point and feeling huge and awkward. Her doctor had given her a requisition for an ultrasound almost two months ago and Claire had finally made the appointment for the week previously but then had to cancel because of her cold. When the doctor examined her on this occasion, he looked a bit concerned and ordered his nurse to schedule an urgent ultrasound. That very afternoon Dan drove her to the clinic for the procedure.

Afterwards the technician approached her with a strange look on his face. "I've called your doctor with the results and he wants you to return to his office now."

"Why? What's wrong?"

"I can't discuss that with you. You will have to ask him."

Claire and Dan drove back to the clinic silently, each preoccupied with ominous worries. They didn't have to wait long before being ushered into the doctor's office together. He was waiting there for them.

"What's wrong?" Dan blurted anxiously.

The doctor looked at them and after a short pause he told them. "You're going to have twins."

Dan and Claire looked at each other in stunned silence. "But are they okay?" Claire asked in a fearful, whispery voice.

"They look pretty healthy on the ultrasound, kicking and moving around."

"How has it taken this long to find out?" Dan asked hoarsely.

"Your wife appears to have been too busy to schedule an ultrasound before now even though I gave her the requisition two months ago."

"I did schedule it for last week but I had a bad cold."

The doctor said nothing.

"But why did the original ultrasound not show it? I understand that Claire was more than three months along when that was done," Dan asked.

"That I can't tell you. Sometimes it happens that way. One fetus is hidden behind the other. We're trying to capture a three dimensional object with a two dimensional image and it doesn't always work in those early months."

Dan and Claire had now had a few minutes to grasp this new reality. They looked at each other and both began laughing in an almost hysterical manner.

The doctor looked bewildered by this response and Dan was quick to explain.

"You would have to have lived our life to understand, Doc. For fifteen years we've been rearing our very disabled daughter, loving her and enjoying her presence in our lives in many ways, but always wondering what it would be like to have a normal child and knowing there was no hope of ever finding out.

Now this. Quite apart from anything else we may be feeling or have yet to feel, the sheer irony of it is just delicious."

That was the longest speech Claire had ever heard Dan make and she knew how hard this had hit him. But she was still in defensive mode, hedging her bets. A lot could go wrong yet. "Are there any special precautions I need to take, Doctor? I know that many twins are born prematurely. How do I guard against that?"

"You have told me you go to the gym regularly. Are you still going?"

"Yes. Should I stop?"

"No! You're quite healthy and actually in better shape now than you were during your last physical check-up, so keep going. Just be very careful not to place any extra strain on your stomach and inform your trainer. From what you've told me about her, she sounds quite competent. She'll know what you should and should not do."

"How about work?" Dan asked. "When should she stop working?"

"It's the same," the doctor said, turning to Claire. "From what you've told me, you enjoy your work and it isn't too physically onerous. Just make sure you eat right and get plenty of sleep. I'll see you again in a week. You'll have to check in with me very regularly now. Make an appointment with the receptionist."

And with that, they were off. It was late afternoon, and since they had help with Jessie, uncharacteristically, Dan drove them directly to Sorrentino's. "We have too much to discuss to go home right now," he said.

They asked for a booth at the restaurant and Dan ordered a shot of whiskey when the server came, also very uncharacteristic of him. Claire ordered green tea.

They sat there then in silence just looking at each other. "What are you thinking?" Claire asked softly.

"I was wondering if it's boys or girls or both. We should have asked."

"I don't want to know. Don't we have enough to think about?" Claire asked, a faint note of irritation in her voice.

Dan grabbed her hand. "Don't look like that, Claire. It's wonderful news!"

"Is it? Have you thought of the expense?"

"Claire, get over it. I know we were kind of poor in the early years, but not anymore. I'm doing very well now and we'll be fine, even without you working."

"Yes, work. How am I ever going to be able to get back to work again with twins? Just think of the babysitting cost!"

"This isn't like you, Claire. What's really bothering you?"

"I'm scared," she replied, hanging her head. "Twins are high risk for prematurity and often one twin does not do as well as the other because of uneven nutrition in the womb."

"But that's why you're trying very hard to eat right and to get enough exercise to keep your oxygen level and general metabolic level up. That's what you've been telling me for months, isn't it?"

"Yes, I suppose." Claire looked at Dan wistfully. "I just can't believe we can be so lucky and have two beautiful babies. Not after Jessie. I'm just scared."

Dan stood up, crossed over to her and put his arms around her. "It's going to be all right. I can *feel* it. It's *our* turn to have some luck!"

He sat down again and Claire smiled. "Maybe you're right. I just don't want to jinx it by being too happy."

"If you don't want to jinx it, just stay out of trouble. How long are you going to keep working?"

"I was planning to just keep going as long as I could but now I don't know. I'm thinking that this will be my last month of work. Hazel is doing really well and I think she's ready to take over. I can always drop by regularly even after I quit just to give advice when needed and help out a bit."

That sounds like a good plan to me. You'll be able to sleep as long as you need in the morning and won't have any pressure on you. You can quit now if you want to."

"No. I feel like I'm okay to keep going for a few weeks more."

When they got home, it was to find that there had been a call from Jimmy. Claire called back immediately, worried about Tia. "Tia's fine," Jimmy said gruffly. "I am on my way over. I'll see you soon."

Dan answered the door when Jimmy arrived, and then stepped aside to allow him to dump the two huge garbage bags he was carrying on the floor. "Keep the door open," Jimmy said. "I'll be back in a minute." Actually, he had to make several trips, lugging in a bassinette, a baby bath, bottles, tiny diapers and other paraphernalia. "Marion should be through with the crib and high chair in a few months and I'll bring those over then," he said.

Dan ushered him in and sat him down with a bottle of beer. "So you've definitely decided?" he asked.

"I decided as soon as this happened," Jimmy said, "but it took a while to convince Tia."

Claire joined them now and thanked Jimmy for the baby materials. "But it's not going to solve all our problems," she said mysteriously.

"Oh?" he asked. "What else do you need? Maybe we have it and I just forgot to bring it over."

"I don't think so," Claire said. "Not unless you can cart over a second load of stuff exactly the same." She paused for a minute and then added dramatically, "We are having twins!"

Dan had a silly grin on his face, waiting for Jimmy's reaction but Jimmy said nothing right away. And when he did speak it was not what they expected to hear.

"Funny how things work out," he said sourly. "We're having no kid and you're having two."

Claire looked at him. She'd never liked this side of Jimmy when it came out but generally she tolerated it. She put it down to his bad experiences with his first wife that appeared to have left him with a permanent chip on his shoulder and she generally just let his negative remarks pass without comment. But not this time!

"Yes, it *is* funny," she said evenly. "You have Mario who is close to being a genius, and Marion who is beautiful and healthy and already quite advanced developmentally. And we have Jessie who is almost completely helpless. And now we're having twins who may or may not be okay and who are not likely to develop as well as either of your children."

For once Jimmy looked embarrassed and he immediately apologized. "Do you want me to tell Tia this news?" he asked.

"I'm not sure," Claire said. "Not if she's going to have the same reaction. "Perhaps we better wait awhile. Maybe we should just keep it between the three of us for the time being." Jimmy and Dan agreed and Jimmy left shortly after.

Dan and Claire just looked at each other when the door closed. Finally Claire said, "He really can't help it. It's his way of coping. Some people just can't help feeling sorry for themselves and being a victim." Dan just shook his head but said nothing.

Chapter 19: Cleaning Up a Loose End

It was now a month since Tia's miscarriage and Claire was finding it increasingly difficult to get out the door in the morning early enough to get to work at 8 o'clock. *Just two weeks of work to go and, boy, am I glad!* Claire thought as she drove carefully down the snow-covered streets.

Hazel was already there when she arrived and had her professional face on. Both Claire and Tia had coached her not to share personal information or past job information with the other staff. By this time they all knew that Hazel would be taking over when Claire left. But the message that both Claire and Tia had drilled into Hazel was that the best way to get the staff on her side was by action, not words.

Fortunately, Tia's predictions had been correct and Hazel had been a natural. She quickly formed comfortable relationships with Roscoe, Bill and Mavis, which after all was the main goal. Claire was especially impressed by how well Mavis had connected with her. *Better than me,* Claire thought grudgingly. *It must be because of all Hazel's work with her younger siblings––from the time she was very young herself.*

Gaining the trust and respect of the other staff members had not been as easy but it seemed to be coming along now. A big question for them was why Claire had found it necessary to bring in someone from outside. Strangely enough, it was not the full time staff who had questioned this nearly as much as the part-time student staff. Claire speculated that it had offended their growing sense of professional identity.

There was another group who questioned her choice of team leader as well, PDD, the funding and monitoring source for the agency that supported her three clients. That's why she had invited her PDD Contract Specialist out today so he could see for himself how Hazel was functioning. To this end, the next hour was largely spent in private conference with Hazel, priming her on how to function when the PDD person was present. But, as it turned out, this was more for Claire's reassurance than Hazel's.

All three clients had remained at home that day since there was no other way for Robert Sawyer, the PDD representative to fairly evaluate Hazel's level of functioning. Claire stationed herself in Bill's leather reclining chair in the living room where she could sit in relative comfort while watching and listening to the proceedings. A clear program schedule was in place and two other staff members were present to assist in carrying it out.

Hazel supervised the staff and their interactions with the clients intermittently while deftly handling the lunch preparation between times. Claire did nothing but explain the odd issue to Robert—for example, the rationale for some of the program ideas she came up with. When Carl, a new staff member, tried to give Mavis a drink she immediately began to choke. The cerebral palsy that affected her made drinking a serious problem. After much experimentation, Claire had found that Mavis could best manage liquids out of a short, capped bottle with a rigid plastic tube attached directly to the cap. The bottle was turned upside down and the liquid gently squeezed into her mouth through the tube at a rate she could tolerate. When this latest bout of choking happened, Hazel asked Dave if she could try and took the bottle from him only when he offered. Then she quietly demonstrated her technique.

"I'm here, Mavis," Hazel said comfortingly, knowing that Mavis would recognize her through her voice. "Let's try this drink again," and she placed the drinking tube gently between her lips, waiting for Mavis to open her mouth in anticipation. Once Mavis indicated she was ready by closing her lips over the tube, Hazel gently tipped the bottle forward, squeezing it softly to let some liquid out. When she gauged that Mavis had taken as much as she safely could without choking, she took the bottle away and waited a minute before trying again.

After two tries, Hazel turned to Carl, the new staff person, and explained in a soft voice, "You have to work with her, watch and kind of gauge her response. You get a feel for it after a while. It's not something that can be taught. Do you want to try now?"

Carl tried then and everyone watching—including Robert—could see that he was carefully copying the technique he'd seen Hazel employing. This time he had much more success. "I think you're a natural at this," Hazel said admiringly. You caught on really quickly!" Carl smiled and Hazel added, "Just remember one thing: there's no hurry. Getting Mavis to drink without choking is really important and a main program goal. It significantly increases her quality of life. So just take your time and don't get impatient." Claire silently nodded her head in agreement.

Robert observed that Hazel's tone was collaborative but firm, kind but not patronizing, and he saw that Carl recognized this and was buying into the program and risking investing himself in order to do a good job. The same dynamics held true when Hazel interceded during staff interactions with the other two clients and he could see that they would be in good hands.

Claire smirked in self-congratulation, forgetting for the moment that Hazel had been Tia's idea, not hers. Out loud, she stated to Robert, "I plan to be here off and on that last month before the babies are born and to come back often afterwards as well. And, of course, Hazel can call me at any time if she has a problem. So are you feeling okay about this transition?"

Robert nodded his head and for good measure added a comment. "I wish staff-client interactions were as sensitive and effective in some of the other homes I supervise." Claire stored that comment away in her heart and as soon as she was able to get away in private, one of her now very frequent bathroom visits, she wrote it down as well as she could remember it, adding the date and the circumstances.

The next time I'm feeling down about myself I'll pull this out, she promised herself.

At home over supper that evening, she regaled Dan with the morning's happening and Robert's reaction. Then she sat back feeling more relaxed than she had in a long time. *It really is going to work out,* she said to herself. *I'm free and everything I have worked for over the past three years will carry on and even get better. I'm really free to think of the future now, of other things.*

However, it was not the upcoming birth of her children that occupied Claire's mind at that moment. It was the unfinished business of Caroline's murder. They were at a dead end—or were they? Had Sylvia been completely forthcoming or not? No wonder McCoy liked her so much! She had that same rigid, stubborn, moralistic quality that he himself possessed. And that lack of flexibility was no way to solve murders. It was time to crack Sylvia's hard, self-righteous shell. Claire needed to know a lot more about Caroline, her past life and any dirty little secrets of hers that Sylvia might be

hiding if she was going to get to the bottom of this—
and she only had a few weeks left to do it!

Chapter 20: Following a Cold Trail

The next morning was Claire's gym session. She had changed her gym time to nine and came in late to the co-op on her gym days. The early morning sessions she'd set up previously were just too hard now. Claire saw Sylvia almost immediately and walked over to her, acting like she hadn't seen her in a long time. "Hi, Sylvia!" she said, in an artificially bright tone. "How *are* you? It's great to see you!" and she reached out her hand. Sylvia grasped it and palmed the message Claire had given her, uttering her own enthusiastic greeting.

A few minutes later, Sylvia sent her a text saying she could spare enough time for coffee at Starbucks after Claire finished her session at 10. But Claire emailed back saying 'no'. What they had to discuss shouldn't be overheard, and other gym staff visited Starbucks as well. Also it would be time-consuming. She asked if they could meet for lunch at Sicilian Pasta Kitchen South at 12 or after. A couple of minutes later, Sylvia typed back saying she had no clients until one that afternoon. Could they meet about 11:15 at the restaurant? That would give them 90 minutes or so which should be long enough. *Perfect! See you there,"* Claire texted back.

Once they settled in at the restaurant and had ordered their drinks, Claire decided to herself that she'd best begin this delicate conversation by channeling Tia. "How are you doing these days, Sylvia?" she asked solicitously. "You look a little tired."

Sylvia gave her a measured look and then responded. "I'm fine but I really have to find a home for Fergus or I'm going to have to take him to the SPCA. I'm just not a cat person and I'm sick of being dragged down by him. *That's* why I'm so tired. I like to go to bed early because I get up early but he's always prowling around until late and doesn't let me sleep." She looked at Claire meaningfully and Claire read her silent message. If she was going to cooperate with Claire then Claire needed to solve her 'Fergus' problem and do it right now.

Claire thought rapidly. That clerk at Chapters she had talked to might take him but she'd have to find the right time to talk to her about it and Sylvia's silent demand was for an immediate answer. *Maybe,* Claire thought to herself, and then in her characteristic way just went ahead and blurted it out. "I can take him to the co-op. I'm sure that Roscoe and Bill and Mavis would really enjoy having him there! I could pick him up from you later today when you get home from work!"

Sylvia looked at her shrewdly. "Are you sure? I have to know that he'll be all right there. I wouldn't want him abused or mishandled. They might hurt him—not deliberately maybe but because they don't know any better ... the way they are. That Roscoe I met, for example. He's a big, clumsy guy. He might trip over Fergus or fall on him or something. And I promised Caroline I'd make sure that Fergus was okay if anything ever happened to her!"

Claire swallowed hard to choke down the outraged response that sprang to her lips. With a silent apology to Roscoe, she responded. "Oh, I don't think so. They are closely supervised at all times and we could even keep Fergus in Mavis' bedroom at night. She certainly can't hurt him since she can't even get out of her chair!"

"We-l-l, if you're sure?" Sylvia replied.

"I'm sure. Do you want me to pick him up later?"

"That would be great!" Sylvia replied, smiling in relief. "Any time after 7:30 would work for me. Now what is it you wanted to talk to me about?"

"We've hit a dead end in our investigation into Caroline's death—and to me that means we're on the wrong track. I think the only thing we can do at this point is to dig deeper into Caroline's background. I know by some of the things you've said that you've carefully edited the material about Caroline you've given us, maybe for a good reason, like to protect her reputation. But she's dead; nothing people say can hurt her anymore. And the only thing left that we can do for her is to give her justice!" Claire tried hard to say this in a kind, understanding voice, wishing Tia was there to defuse her intensity. But at the same time, Claire realized that this was something she had to do herself. The gentle approach had not worked!

Sylvia just looked at her and said in her prim voice "I told you everything about Caroline that could possibly be relevant to finding her killer. I don't see why it's necessary to completely strip her of her dignity!"

"And that's just the trouble," Claire said. "You don't see! I've solved or played a significant role in solving six murders in the past few years so I think I can see what you can't!" Claire took a deep breath. She was getting worked up and if Tia had been there she would have told her to cool it.

"What do you want to know?" Sylvia asked in an annoyed tone of voice.

"Everything!" Claire said. "What were her parents like? What happened to her after they died and before she started working at the gym? Who else did she ever go out with other than the ex you told me about? How did she do at school? Did she ever get in trouble with the authorities?"

Sylvia said nothing for a couple of minutes and Claire, having been well trained by Tia, sat there silently and waited. Finally, Sylvia looked at her and said, "There is one big thing. I don't know how it could possibly be related—but Caroline's mother was an alcoholic and she drank while she was pregnant with her."

"So that must be her mother in the picture!"

"Yes," Sylvia said. "I'm thinking that's who it was, and I'm pretty sure that's her husband with her. Caroline showed me another picture of her parents once."

"What about the ones in the other picture?" Claire asked. "Is that them, too?"

"Yes, I think so. They were younger then. Caroline told me they'd bought a house or were about to close a deal on one and that's why they look so happy there!"

"Did they ever get the house?"

"I don't know."

"I don't think they did—and I think I know the reason why." Sylvia raised her eyebrows interrogatively. "Later," Claire said. "Let's get back to the alcohol issue. Did Caroline ever get diagnosed with Fetal Alcohol Spectrum Disorder?"

"Yes, when she was in grade school," Sylvia replied in a low voice.

"And you never thought that was important to tell us?"

"No. Why should it be? I'm pretty sure she didn't get murdered because of that."

"Really? What do you know about FAS-D? Do you know how people can look and act in a way that seems perfectly normal when all the time they're suffering from poor judgment, difficulty planning and organizing effectively, poor impulse control, lack of insight—and I could go on. Did you know that our jails are filled with people, many of them undiagnosed, who are suffering from the effects of prenatal alcohol consumption by their mothers? Do you not think that this might have caused Caroline to make some bad choices in her life, get mixed up with the wrong people and upset some dangerous people in the process? It would have been really helpful to know this little gem of information months ago—and I'm sure McCoy will feel the same!"

Sylvia said nothing but shifted uncomfortably in her seat.

"Okay," Claire said, jotting notes down in a little book as she spoke. "Tell me what happened after Caroline's parents died. What were her foster parents like and what's the real reason her relatives didn't take her in?"

"She just said that her foster parents weren't the least bit interested in her. They were totally focused on their own two younger children and she was only there for the extra income she generated. As to why her relatives didn't take her in, I already told you. They thought she would be a bad influence on their own daughter."

"Yeah, sure—but why? They must have had a reason for thinking that. What happened at school? Did she ever get in trouble with the authorities?"

Sylvia looked very uncomfortable. After a long pause, she muttered, "Well, she did say that she often got into trouble for lifting things."

"Lifting things? You mean she stole things from others?" Claire clarified.

"Yeah, but nothing that big or important. She mentioned a girlfriend's scarf that she really liked and sometimes she nicked a little cash from her foster mom's purse because she said they never gave her enough spending money."

"Did she ever regret that, feel bad about it?"

"No, I think she felt justified because she had so little and her parents had died and left her with nothing."

"It's that kind of thinking that is exactly why a lot of those people I mentioned before are in jail. Did she shoplift? Anything significant? Did she ever get charged?"

Sylvia said nothing for a full minute. Finally she muttered rather sulkily, "Yes, yes, and yes."

"What was it, the big thing?"

"A pair of $400.00 ski boots. She was really into skiing at one point."

"Was this before or after she turned 18?"

"Just a few months before but she was charged as a juvenile."

"So was her record sealed?"

"Yes. But her uncle knew about it because she had to ask him for bail money. And he told his wife, even though Caroline didn't want him to do that."

"What about the school situation? How far did she get? What were her marks like? Was she ever in trouble?"

"She failed twice and was in grade ten when she dropped out. She was 18 at that point and her social worker was trying to put together some kind of support package for her so she could finish school, even though she had aged out of the child welfare system. But late one night, she just packed up her stuff, called a taxi and sneaked out of her foster parent's home. She had arranged a room at the YWCA and stayed there for a few days until her money ran out."

"What happened then?"

"She was sitting in a bar that last night wondering where she was going to get the money to pay for her next night's lodging, when this older guy came up and started talking to her. She'd had a couple of drinks at that point and just blurted out her troubles to him. He immediately offered to take her in, no strings attached. She considered her options and decided it had to be better than ending up on the street. So they went back to her room at the Y and she packed up her stuff and moved in with him that very night. She stayed with him for four years."

"Wow!" What was their—er—relationship like?"

"Well, for the first couple of nights he was very respectful. Then on the third night he came into her room. She didn't resist him. She figured at that point that she didn't have much to lose."

"Okay, why did she leave and where is this guy now? This might be a lead!"

"His name is Eduardo Montoya. He would be close to 50 now and he came here from El Salvador many years ago because of the political unrest there. His brother 'disappeared' and his father was tortured and died in prison. His mother passed away a few months afterward, 'died of a broken heart' he told Caroline. It did something to him, Caroline said. He didn't trust anyone or connect to anyone here. The only reason he ever talked to her in the first place was because she seemed so weak and helpless and therefore unthreatening. And, of course, he was lonely, here all on his own and cut off from family and country."

"He was very good to her. He did have a good job. He was an electrician in his own country and was able to get a job with a big electrical company here that paid well and had benefits. He paid for Caroline to take classes and get her fitness certification and then take extra specialist courses on top of that—which is why she ended up at that fitness seminar in Detroit where she witnessed the murder. Anyway, after a while, Caroline got settled. She got a good job at a gym and started meeting people. She was bored with Eduardo so one day while he was at work she just packed up her stuff and moved out. Caroline said that she left him a nice note and thanked him for everything but explained that it was time she moved on with her life."

"She never felt bad about leaving him, never wondered how this would affect him?"

"No, she didn't seem to."

"Of course, she didn't. And that, by the way, is typical of the FAS-D brain. She didn't think of consequences or what her effect on other people would be. She didn't really understand such concepts as loyalty and gratitude. And that, of course, is why she went around bragging and stepping on people's toes at the gym without ever thinking how others would be affected or react. Do you understand now why this information is important in terms of tracking down her killer?"

Sylvia nodded her head mutely.

"Do you have an address for this man or do you know where he works?"

"All Caroline said was that he worked for a company called Adonis Electric. She got a kick out of the name because Adonis was the mortal lover of the Greek goddess, Aphrodite, and she wondered if he'd been 'electrifying' to be able to win her love."

"I guess I can track him down from there," was all Claire replied. At this point, the last thing she was interested in was Caroline's peculiar sense of humor. She consulted her notes to see what other points she had missed and returned to the school issue. "Did Caroline connect with any guys while she was at school?"

"Yes, she mentioned a guy named Donnie or something. I wasn't listening too closely when she talked about him."

"And how serious was *that* relationship?"

"According to Caroline he liked her a lot and even talked about getting married at some point in the future. But after a while, she got bored with him and moved on. She was quite attractive and she knew it. She described herself as a bit of a flirt—and I'd say it was probably more than 'a bit'! She also implied that she slept around quite a lot while she was in high school, even junior high."

"It all fits," Claire said. Without any parental guidance she didn't have a chance—and even with the best parents in the world, her chances would have been slim with that kind of a brain."

At some point during this marathon conversation, they had ordered and eaten a simple lunch. It was nearing one o'clock and Sylvia said she needed to leave. Claire said good-bye and then sat there a while longer with a piece of the restaurant's signature raspberry cream pie for company. She figured she deserved it after all that! But she used her alone time to contemplate her next move. She regretfully decided that given her condition and Tia's still fragile mental state, she'd have to involve McCoy.

After some further thought, Claire picked up her phone and called the detective. He answered immediately. "I have some further information and it's too complicated to relay over the phone. May I come and see you now?"

"Fine. Come as soon as you like."

"About a half hour?" she said and hung up the phone. Then she got busy organizing and recopying the salient points of her conversation with Sylvia. She made asterisks where she thought that further follow-up was warranted and once she had one neat package for McCoy, she packed up her bag, paid the bill and left.

Chapter 21: An Awkward Meeting and New Directions

Inspector McCoy looked very shocked when Claire walked into his office. She had expected this reaction and prepared her opening remarks in advance. "It happened before," she blurted. "I just hadn't realized—and it's twins to boot!"

"Oh! Er—congratulations—I guess. You *are* happy about it, I assume?"

"It took some getting used to but now Dan and I are both looking forward to it."

McCoy smiled and nodded his head. "Then I'm happy for you, Claire," he said, some of the old softness returning to his voice. "You deserve to have some children you don't—er—have to struggle with so much."

Claire gave him full marks for diplomacy. He had come a long way towards understanding and accepting 'differently abled' people', as the currently popular euphemism would put it. She got down to business then, handing him the copy of the notes she'd made for him and going over the most salient points. "By the way, Sylvia is my contact person at the gym."

McCoy raised his eyebrows in a questioning way and Claire went on to explain.

"I overheard another trainer talking to her one day and saying that Sylvia was the one who'd been closest to Caroline so who did she think might have murdered her. After that, I contrived a way to connect with Sylvia and to get her to feed me information. The trouble is I could tell she was always holding back. She had some notion that she needed to protect Caroline's memory and she only told me what *she* thought was relevant to solving the murder. I met with her today and insisted that she tell me everything and that's how I got this new material which, as you can see, suggests several possible leads."

Claire sat back after making this long speech, feeling simultaneously a little guilty for throwing Sylvia under the bus, but at the same pleased that this would surely help to deflate McCoy's exalted opinion of her and remind him of who his real source of support in murder investigations was. However, she was to be disappointed.

"I can understand why Sylvia felt that way and I respect that," McCoy said in that same soft tone of voice he had previously reserved for Claire in the few special moments when they had felt close to each other. Claire gritted her teeth but said nothing.

McCoy scanned over the material Claire had given him and said, almost grudgingly, "There *may* be a couple of leads here. I won't really know until we can follow up on them. And by '*we*' I mean the police department, not *you!*" he said to Claire in a warning tone.

This was too much for her, following so closely on her recent setback in terms of regaining her top dog, informal consultancy position. Claire sniped back, "If I thought I could handle it on my own in my present condition, I would never have shared this information with you—but I can't. Therefore, I'll have to trust you to follow up on it, despite your lack of progress so far on this case!" Claire suddenly wished Tia had been there to stop her from saying this and she braced for the inevitable blowback—but she was to be pleasantly surprised.

"That's my old Claire," he said softly. "I was wondering where she'd gone!"

Claire sat back stunned and then experienced a moment of clarity. She finally understood what Tia had been telling her, an idea she'd previously dismissed as sentimental drivel. "If you want to relate authentically to somebody else you must first relate authentically to yourself." Claire took this to mean that it was time to bravely face down the elephant in the room. She summoned up her courage and proceeded.

"Look," she said. "You and I have always had a difficult relationship. I can't completely respect your rigid, methodical, unimaginative approach to crime solving and you certainly don't value my spontaneous, intuitive approach. We are very different but what we have in common is that we both want these murders solved and are prepared to work as hard as possible to get that done. Would you agree?"

McCoy nodded his head but said nothing and Claire went on.

"And whatever weird thing has been happening between us, I think it's due to that, that we respect each other but can't quite respect each other and that we want to work together but can't trust each other enough to work together—and it creates tension that we have to address somehow."

McCoy nodded his head again but shifted uncomfortably in his chair, and Claire knew that she was hitting a little too close to the bone.

"I need to get this murder out of the way before the babies are born and I have to retreat within the four walls of my house to focus exclusively on them for a time. And I know you won't be happy until we have tracked down the killer. Can we please start working together again?"

"McCoy just looked at her but said nothing. Claire sat back waiting for an answer and finally he said, "We can try."

"Okay!" Claire said, leaning forth eagerly in her chair. "What do you find most relevant in the notes I gave you? Where would your starting point be?"

"I'm glad you uncovered the fact of Caroline's Fetal Alcohol Syndrome."

Claire was pleased about this and didn't think it was the time to bring him up to speed on the latest nomenclature. "What you had to say about how it can affect people is really helpful. As you say, we have to do some further digging into Caroline's life and who she may have upset along the way. This could lead to some totally new lines of investigation. I'm going to start by talking to Sylvia myself, to see if she has any more information about how Caroline lived the last few years of her life that might lead us to a new suspect or suspects."

"She told me you were collaborating directly with her and preferred her approach to mine, found her easier to work with," Claire blurted, and then blushed furiously. She'd been holding this in for a long time and was relieved to finally get it out but now felt a crippling sense of embarrassment.

"There is only one Claire," he said softly, and she had to be content with that.

Desperately anxious now to get them back on a professional footing, Claire said assertively, "I think we need to start with this Eduardo guy but I also think we need to find out whoever this Donnie character is that Caroline was involved with at school. Maybe you can get Sergeant Crombie to go through the high school yearbooks and interview any of the teachers there who were present when Caroline was a student."

"Good idea; I'll get right onto that!" he said, a note of sarcasm in his voice, and just like that the old tension between them was back.

"I had a feeling it was too good to last," Claire said cheekily, and was rewarded for her gall by a rare, spontaneous grin on McCoy's part.

Chapter 22: McCoy Takes Charge

Claire met with Inspector McCoy again a week later
but she knew that this would be one of the last times.
She was finding it increasingly difficult to fit behind the
steering wheel of her car and next week was her last
week at work. After that, if McCoy still wanted to
collaborate he'd have to come to the house.

"Sergeant Crombie went through the school
yearbooks and interviewed the teachers, as you
suggested," he said. Claire rolled her eyes. After all
they'd been through together you'd think they'd be on a
first name basis by now.

"He found three Donnies or Donalds," the inspector
continued, one in grade 10, one in 11 and one in 12.
The 10th grader had the most classes in common with
Caroline but he was two years younger than her.
Crombie was able to track him down but that Donald
had nothing to do with Caroline of any significance.
This kid described her with a kind of awe as 'beautiful
and sophisticated' and it was clear that he regarded her
as far out of his league."

"What about the other two?" Caroline asked.

"The 11th grader shared a drama class with Caroline.
He has since graduated, of course, and is working at a
Home Hardware store. Crombie was able to track him
down there. Anyway, he did say that he remembered
Caroline from that class. He even admitted having a
little crush on her but said it never went anywhere. His
recollection was that she was always flirting with other

guys and involved in one intense relationship after another—or even at the same time."

"Hmm, you can imagine the girls who would have hated her guts. I wonder if your Sergeant Crombie should check on some of them?"

"No, I don't see the point," McCoy said. "Difficult to believe someone would be holding a grudge about a high school flirtation or even if Caroline moved in on somebody else's boyfriend after all these years."

"I suppose so," Claire said, not quite believing in the injured girlfriend theory herself. "So does Sergeant Crombie think there's any point in following up further with this guy or not?"

"No. He's pretty satisfied with his story."

"And the 12th grader? What about him?"

"Well, that's a little more interesting. The other two both mentioned him when they were asked if they knew of anyone Caroline had connected with at school. Apparently he did definitely go out with her, at least a few times, but we've been unable to track him down."

"What about his parents? Can't they help?"

"Apparently the whole family moved away at some point and nobody seems to know where they went."

"Well, haven't you got a system, a network you can use to track the family."

"Sure—for criminals. But it's not much good if you aren't a criminal! We're going to keep trying though," he added. "It's too good a lead to pass up."

"Okay. What about this Eduard Montoya guy? Have you found him?"

"Not yet. He's moved from where he lived when Caroline was with him."

"Well, have you checked on what Caroline was doing during that time? She spent four years with him and spent some of the time in classes, sure—but what did she do the rest of the time? Have you checked with the gyms to see if anybody remembers her that far back and, if so, do they recall who she hung out with during that period?"

"No, we haven't—but that's not a bad idea," McCoy said musingly.

Their interview ended then and Claire returned to work but not for long. Soon she was experiencing some pretty severe contractions and she called Dan for advice as to what to do. Having established that they were quite far apart and not at regular intervals, he replied, "Just sit tight or lie down and I'll be there as soon as I can make it!"

Claire, of course, didn't follow these directions. It was always comforting to receive directions from people who cared about her and were concerned about her but that's all such advice did for her. It gave her a sense of comfort, security, and stability. Now, knowing that Dan was on his way, she set about collecting all the items she had lugged over to the co-op during the past three years to create a more homelike atmosphere during her tenure there.

There was her special reading lamp and coffee cup, a comfy old cardigan and lap throw, a pair of slippers, a pillow, some reading material and even a footstool that she sometimes used. She placed them all neatly at the door for Dan to lug out. Because Claire knew that once she left today, she wouldn't be back again except for visits. After she had done this, Claire walked slowly around the house, visiting every room and even the basement, much to Hazel's concern given her condition. She stopped at various points, remembering scattered memories from the past, and when she finally finished and sat down sedately in Bill's leather recliner that his cousin, Hilda, had given him after the death of her husband and mother, she had tears in her eyes conflicting with a small smile of anticipation as she wondered what the future would hold.

Claire remained in the hospital overnight and the next morning the doctor on call came in to speak to Claire. Fortunately, Dan was also there at the time. "The contractions you've been experiencing are called Braxton-Hicks, otherwise known as 'false labor'. They have slowed significantly since you came in yesterday and should occur only intermittently after this as long as you maintain a more tranquil lifestyle and remain well hydrated. In other words, it doesn't mean you're going into labor yet but even if you did, it wouldn't be as serious as if it had happened a month ago. You're almost into your ninth month now but the longer you can hold off delivering, the better for those twins of yours."

"Whew. *That's* good news!" Claire exclaimed. It was obvious she'd been quite worried and Dan looked very relieved as well. "I've made the decision not to return to work just so I can relax more and sleep in in the morning if I need to—but what about exercising?"

"You can go to the gym if you feel up to it but if you know how to do the exercises safely without supervision at home that might be a better alternative."

"I do and I will. The thought of just being able to relax and do things at my own speed really appeals to me right now."

"Just don't get too relaxed. Some movement is good," the doctor warned, and Claire nodded her head in agreement. Claire and Dan left the hospital soon after, and she walked in the door of her house knowing that she wouldn't be leaving it again very often for the next few months.

Chapter 23: Home-based Practice

Claire didn't knit or crochet or sew. She washed clothes but depended heavily on the drier since she only ironed when absolutely necessary, usually about once a year. Claire enjoyed cooking and sometimes baking, although her tendency to alter recipes and take short cuts often got her into trouble in that area. She washed dishes and cleaned the kitchen and bathroom as needed but detested vacuuming and dusting. In other words, she was not very domestic.

As she sat at her kitchen table with a second cup of coffee the next morning, she went through her check-list of what would be needed when she brought two infants home from the hospital sometime in the near future. Fortunately, Tia had been generously gifted with many infant clothes and supplies at the time of Marion's birth from various friends, relatives and well-wishers, and since Claire was the lucky recipient of these, she had no concerns there. As for the doubling up issue, one baby bath was enough and they'd been able to acquire a second bassinet from another friend who no longer needed it. This friend had also given her a generously-sized chest of drawers and a baby change table and they could wait a bit to worry about acquiring cribs and a double stroller. Claire had decided that she wasn't going to be one of those moms who carted their baby—babies in this case—around everywhere.

Having satisfied herself that she and Dan were more or less prepared for the upcoming event—not that she would object to being escorted on an occasional trip through the baby sections of a couple of stores—Claire turned her mind to the other matter pressing on her, Caroline's murder.

Could the third Donnie be the one? she asked herself. *What other possible options were there? I must follow up with McCoy about Eduardo. What about Stan Polansky's son? I must ask McCoy exactly what his alibi is and if they've checked any further into whether or not he knew Caroline.* At this point in her ruminations, Claire gave up and called Inspector McCoy.

"Yes, Claire," he said when he answered the phone. "I know you're going to ask me about Eduardo. Crombie did manage to find him and talk to him. He's happily married now and has two young children. Also, he has fond memories of Caroline. He says that if it weren't for her, he never would have come out of his shell. Eduardo had told Caroline that he enjoyed dancing very much when he was a young man in El Salvador and had become quite good at it. She's the one who then dragged him out to dances and showed him where all the best and liveliest dance venues were in Edmonton. He carried on going to those dance places after Caroline left him and that's where he met his wife. Crombie doesn't believe he's good for Caroline's murder."

"I guess I'll have to be satisfied with that. Thank you for sharing," Claire said. "Also, it fits with what Caroline said about him to Sylvia, that he was a gentle person and a chronically fearful person, not exactly the murdering type."

"I've seen all types," McCoy said tersely. "But I agree with you. It's time to pursue other leads—if we had any."

"What about the third Donald?"

"Still no news as to where he's at, but Crombie did find out one tidbit from a former classmate, Reggie something or other. He told Crombie that it was Donald who dumped Caroline, not the other way around. And by the end of his senior year, Donald was closely involved with another girl. Reggie heard that they married a couple of years later."

Claire groaned. "That also doesn't sound too promising! What are we left with? Oh, yeah. What about Ronald Polansky's alibi? And where did *he* go to school?"

"It seems pretty sound. He was at a bar late the night Caroline died. He was there until it closed and he was ordering hard drinks and slurring his words pretty badly. That didn't usually happen with him so the bartender who was there at the time thinks he was pretty loaded and would have needed to go home to sleep it off. And his landlady confirms that she heard somebody clomping up the stairs to the Polansky suite about one in the morning. Neither she nor the neighbors saw or heard anybody leaving the house early the next morning and the coroner has confirmed that Caroline must have been killed between 4 a.m. and the time you reported arriving there at 6."

Claire groaned. I just *know* there's something we're missing. This pregnancy has really done a number on me. I can't use any of my usual techniques!"

"Well, you haven't been entirely crippled by it, have you?"

"What do you mean?" Claire asked defensively.

"It *was* you who broke into Caroline's apartment that first time, right? And before you answer, remember that we agreed to *share information!"*

Claire hesitated for a moment and then agreed. "Fine!" she said. "But we didn't do any harm." McCoy snickered.

"You and Sylvia, right?"

"Yes, me and Sylvia."

"And you did find something, right?"

"Yes."

"What?"

"An old address book."

"And what else?"

Claire didn't answer for a full minute, weighing the pros and cons in her mind. Finally she said, almost in a whisper, "Just a small key".

"May I have that key, please?"

"No, I got rid of it!" she said hastily.

"It wouldn't happen to be the key to a safety deposit box in a bank, would it?"

Claire gulped. "I wouldn't know." Then she added, in the interests of verisimilitude, "It had some strange numbers on it but I don't know what they meant."

"Do you remember the numbers?"

"No, that was a while ago."

"Would you like to know the reason I'm asking you about this?"

"I guess," Claire said cautiously, hoping she wasn't walking into a trap.

"There was a very strange incident recently in a Balmoral-Truett Bank on the north side of the city. There was a sudden electrical blackout in the bank and immediate area. And just before that, this rather odd looking, seemingly older woman staged an apparent heart attack but by the time the lights came back, on she was gone. Then there's the way that Sylvia mysteriously produced a copy of Caroline's will immediately after that. I'm thinking—because just like you, I *am* capable of thinking laterally at times—that the two incidents are connected. And it very much sounds like your handiwork!"

"The will is real!" Claire blurted. "If you checked it against the other copy in the lawyer's office then you'd know that!"

"Yes, but how did you know what lawyer's office to even look in? There are many lawyers in Edmonton."

"Caroline probably told Sylvia what lawyer she had."

"If she didn't tell Sylvia about the will, which according to Sylvia she didn't, then ..."

"But it says right in the will who the lawyer was— and if Caroline gave Sylvia that package of papers then..."

"*If,* and that's a big if!"

"Look, I'll tell you one thing. Even if there was some involvement on my part, and I'm not saying there was, Sylvia had absolutely nothing to do with it!"

"I believe you," McCoy said, almost cheerfully.

"Why?" Claire asked, surprised by his response.

"Because the whole caper sounds too hare-brained and too gutsy. That's not at all like the Sylvia I've been talking to. What I *would* like to know is who else was working with you? The computer system for that grid of the city crashed. There must have been some hacker involved with considerable computer expertise."

"And why would *I* know somebody like that? I can barely open the mail on my computer!"

"Which is precisely why this had to be a team effort," McCoy said smugly. "And I need to find that hacker. That level of ability in someone on the loose is dangerous."

Claire felt a cold chill go down her back and experienced a sudden warning contraction. *I have to calm down,* she said to herself. *This tension is not good for me.*

"Look," Claire said. "Just because I might cut a few corners at times doesn't mean that I'm not a moral person. Just like I told you that Sylvia was not involved, I would do the same for anybody else who might have been involved—so don't even ask!"

"Okay, but I'm still concerned about this hacker running around on the loose."

"Was there any malicious damage done to the bank?" Claire asked. "No! And if this person might be the person I'm thinking of, I can tell you that he's very upright and would never harm or exploit anyone—or pursue technically illegal methods of attaining a worthwhile and moral end if there were any other way!"

"Well," McCoy drawled. "This has been a very interesting and educational conversation. I have a meeting coming up so I'll say good-bye for now. We will leave this issue for the time being."

"But!" Claire croaked, a panicky note in her voice.

"Don't worry about it for the time being, Claire. I *know* who you are. You may have the most cock-eyed, off-base judgment about how to handle certain situations at times but, from all I have seen, your people judgment is excellent!" After a pause he added, "I'll be in touch if I find out anything more that might be useful in terms of tracking down the murderer and please call me if you can figure out any new leads." And with that he hung up the phone.

Claire sat there for a minute, her head in her hands and her heart racing. She wished Tia was home to talk to but she wasn't and there was nobody else she dared confide in. *I just never get away with anything,* she muttered to herself. *I might as well quit trying!*

After a few more quiet moments of self-recrimination, Claire looked around her still cluttered kitchen and went into restitution mode. *I will not think about this anymore,* she said to herself. *I will clean the kitchen. I will clean the whole house. I will become a model citizen and a doting mother so when I get hauled off to prison, Dan and Jessie will have something positive to remember about me and he can tell the babies what a good person their mother was.* A little voice inside her head told her she might be getting carried away and she shook herself and got to work.

Chapter 24: A New Kind of Claire

When Dan came home that evening, he found the house in better order than it had been for a while and there was even a still warm apple pie waiting for him. He greeted Claire with a big kiss and said ,"I'm really going to enjoy having you home and spending all your attentions on us. I have missed that!"

The next two weeks continued in much the same vein with Claire being very domestic and dutiful, always finding something to clean, fix or straighten so everything would be ready for the new babies when they came home and she could just focus on them. Then one morning she woke up in a different frame of mind and the old rebellion set back in.

Sitting at the kitchen table after Dan left, Claire had her second cup of coffee and reviewed her notebook about Caroline's murder. There must be something she was missing! She went over in her mind the various events and her past conversations with Sylvia. Was there anything else Claire had been told by Sylvia about Caroline's life that could provide a clue? There was something, something she had said—but Claire couldn't quite remember it. And the babies would be arriving in another two weeks, assuming she could make it to term.

Claire moved from the kitchen to the living room with yet another cup of coffee and a warmed up piece of the apple cake that Tia had brought over yesterday. She slowly sipped the fragrant coffee and savored the sweet spiciness of the cake while at the same time trying to flip through her notebook on Caroline's murder without greasing up the pages. *I've almost got it,* she muttered to herself—but just then she had a sharp contraction. *I better sit still until it passes* she thought. I don't want to trigger anything.

The contraction passed but only to be followed by another one a couple of minutes later and then another. Claire was getting worried now. As far as Claire's doctor could tell, she was now at 37 weeks gestation. Full term is 40 weeks but mothers carrying twins rarely make it that long and anything after 36 weeks is considered to be within the safe range. All of these thoughts were swarming around in Claire's head as she tried to convince herself that she was experiencing false labor pains. But at the same time another track in her brain was pursuing an elusive memory or set of memories. She almost had it and whatever had happened she needed to get this settled now.

Claire phoned Sylvia to ask her a couple of questions. It took longer than anticipated to get the answers from her because Claire had to stop talking when the contractions got really bad. Sylvia was, of course, concerned and took longer than necessary to review her memories and provide the answers in Claire's opinion..

It's beginning to fit! Claire thought to herself after she hung up the phone and between contractions. They were slowing down now and she hoped to have time to make the second call necessary to confirm her growing suspicions. But just then the phone rang.

When Claire answered the phone it was to hear Sergeant Crombie's voice at the other end. "Oh, Michael! I was just about to call you!"

"*Were* you now! And why might that be?"

But just then Claire had another contraction and could only gasp out a few words. "First, why are you calling me?" She hoped he could not detect her tortured breathing over the phone.

"I was checking to see when those twins might be joining us?"

"Any time now," Claire managed to respond but couldn't elaborate.

"Good! I'm looking forward to meeting them!" After a pause, he went on, "We haven't heard anything from you lately and I was wondering if you were lying doggo! Donald told me about the last conversation he had with you. I must say, that bank caper sounds pretty slick. You would have made a good criminal, you know."

"So I've been told," Claire managed to respond, a slightly sour note in her voice. She was aware of an ego boost but just then another contraction hit and she gasped."

"Is something wrong?" Michael Crombie asked, concern in his voice.

"I seem to be having a few labor pains but they'll probably pass—I hope."

"Oh, my. I better talk quick. I knew you must be worrying about what Donald had to say about your computer hacker." Claire thought about denying her involvement again but decided there was no point. Michael went on, "I don't think he's interested in following through on it. He's just going to let that part of the investigation die. Partly, I know he wants to protect you but he also believes you wouldn't associate with somebody who had malicious intentions. I just wanted to let you know that because I had a feeling when we didn't hear from you for so long that you may have been stewing over it. After all these murder investigations we've been through together, you're almost one of us now and we protect our own. And I know Donald feels that way, too—apart from anything else." Michael finished his speech at that point, leaving Claire to make what she would of that last vague remark.

"Thank you, Michael!" Claire said huskily. "Thank you *so* much!" and he must have realized at that point that the situation had really been bothering her. Claire went on then, "I've been thinking about Caroline's murder". She gasped again as another contraction hit her. After a minute passed she continued, sharing what Sylvia had had to say in their most recent conversation and asking him to check up on two additional matters for her. Claire's contractions were now so severe that she knew it was time to hang up and seek some assistance.

Claire could only think to call Dan and when he answered the phone, she could hardly get the words out between pains to tell him. "Claire, do you think you can wait until I get there? It'll take me at least 20 minutes."

"I—I don't know. It's getting pretty bad. They're close together now."

"I'm calling an ambulance!" he said. "I'll meet you at the hospital!" Within five minutes, Claire heard the siren. She stumbled up from the chair and retrieved her hospital bag, coat, purse and keys. But when she opened the door to let the paramedics in, she doubled up with a pain worse than any of her previous contractions. They quickly loaded her onto a gurney, grabbed her things and locked the door. And then they were on their way, siren blaring.

The emergency room doctor took a quick look at Claire and sent her directly to the delivery room where, following his call, a team was getting prepped to receive her. Dan arrived moments later but had to wait outside the room as there was no time to get him scrubbed and garbed. Five minutes later, a nurse came out to him holding the first baby and a couple of minutes after that, the on-call obstetrician came out holding the second one. There had been no time for her regular obstetrician to get there, but he arrived now and the babies were whisked away for his examination.

Ten minutes later, the babies were brought to Claire and Dan in the recovery room. A nurse was holding one and Claire's obstetrician held the other. Claire looked at him anxiously. "They're fine as far as I can tell at this point, Claire, but we're going to put them in the intensive care nursery for a bit just to be on the safe side." He held one baby close to Claire's hand for her to greet and then passed him over to Dan. The nurse then did the same with the other one while the obstetrician deftly retrieved the first. "You have a boy and a girl!" he informed them. They are fraternal twins, and he motioned for the nurse to take them away and place them under the special lamps in the neo-natal intensive care nursery.

The obstetrician stayed with them a few minutes longer, knowing that the newborns were in good hands with the highly specialized and experienced neo-natal intensive care nurse in charge of the unit. "I'm sorry I couldn't make it here in time to deliver your babies, Claire. How close together were the contractions when you called the ambulance?"

"Uh, 90 seconds, I guess. Dan called them."

The obstetrician frowned. "Didn't I ask you to leave for the hospital when they were three to five minutes apart?"

"Yes, but I was in the middle of something very important. I simply had to finish it before leaving?"

Dr. Falkes looked at Dan who simply raised his eyebrows. "It's who she is," he said with a shrug. "I can't control her."

"But they're going to be okay, aren't they?" Claire asked, turning worried eyes to the doctor. "What about the weight? You said one was smaller, and I know they're premature. Will the small one be delayed?"

"Have you been following Dr. Google?" he asked. "First of all, most twins are born by this stage. The womb simply can't sustain all that weight any longer. Secondly, the 4-ounce difference between them, given their birth weight levels, is not that significant." A nurse had come in to give him that information and he told them now. The boy is 5 pounds 4 ounces and the girl is 5 pounds 8 ounces, and that's actually pretty good for twins born at 37 weeks. Also, their births were quick and relatively easy so I don't think they suffered any birth trauma. We can't give definitive answers at this stage, of course, but I'd say all the signs are good."

Claire gave him a grateful smile and he asked, "Have you decided on any names yet?"

Dan started to shake his head when Claire answered: Isaac and Isabella—Ike and Izzie for short."

Both men looked surprised and Dan said, "Claire and I will have to discuss this a little further. Nothing is decided for sure yet," and he gave Claire a meaningful look.

Chapter 25: Split Focus

The next week was a very busy one. Claire and the babies remained in the hospital but by the end of the week, it was obvious they were all fit to go home.

The nurses were probably happy to see the last of them because of the parade of visitors that had hogged the viewing windows of the nursery, cluttered up the waiting room and Claire's room and clogged the hallway in between.

One of those visitors had been Sergeant Michael Crombie. Inspector McCoy had chosen not to come for reasons of his own. When Michael arrived, Claire shooed everyone else out of her room, stating that she needed to meet with him in private.

"Well?" she asked. "What have you found out?"

"I just assumed from the way the bartender talked that Ronald had been sitting at the bar the night before Caroline was killed. But that's not what happened. He came *up* to the bar to order his drink but he was actually sitting at a table in the back corner. One of the other staff saw him there that night and thought it was unusual. He generally sat at the bar—alone. But this night he was back at that table with a woman. It was very dark so the staff member couldn't tell me anything about her, not even the color of her hair for sure, but he said it was definitely a woman. They both had glasses in front of them, Ronald with his usual beer but the woman was drinking gin and tonic. He could tell because he saw the slice of lime in her glass."

"You need to find out who that girl is. Did you ask him?"

"No. Ronald happened to come into the bar the night after I talked to the bartender the second time and he told him I'd been back. Ronald told his father who phoned the inspector and complained about harassment. Donald told me to leave it alone because he had a solid enough alibi and it *did* look like harassment."

Claire gritted her teeth. "Did you follow up on my idea about the school?"

"Yes, and that was interesting. Ronald Polansky *did* attend Caroline's school. He's pretty low profile in the yearbooks but his school picture is there for all three high school years and —get this! In one of the picture captions his name is written as Ronald (Ronnie) Polansky!"

"I *knew* it!" Claire said triumphantly. But before she could ask any more questions of Michael, there was a knock on the door and Dan stepped in. Their 'business talk' then came to an abrupt end since the last thing Claire wanted was for Dan to know how involved she still was with this mystery.

"Guess what?" Dan said. "I just ran into your doctor down the hall and he said you and the babies can leave this afternoon if you like!"

"Of *course,* I like!" Claire said, all smiles.

Michael Crombie greeted Dan and then got up to go. "I'll get out of your way then so you can get ready. Oh! I almost forgot. Donald sent you these." He pulled two tiny gold id bracelets from his pocket. One was inscribed with *Ike* and the other with *Izzie.* "He said to tell you he liked your choice of names. He said it was so Claire!" Claire grinned. This unique gift meant more to her than she was prepared to let on to either Michael or her husband.

The next hour passed in a blur as Claire dressed, packed and got the babies ready to face their first taste of an Edmonton winter. Dan warmed up the car well and then parked it right in the front entrance driveway area of the hospital. Claire sat in the assigned wheelchair and held Isaac carefully in her lap. A nurse guided her chair out to the car with Dan walking beside them carrying Isabella.

Dan fastened both babies into their backward facing car seats in the back bench seat of their Volkswagen Eurovan and then helped Claire to settle in the front seat. The middle row of seats had been removed to accommodate Jessie's wheelchair and Claire felt very far removed from the babies. She wanted to somehow crawl in and sit between them for the short ride home but it was just impossible in her present weakened and sore condition. She had to be content with keeping her head permanently cranked around so she could at least see the backs of their heads whenever the car turned a corner at a certain angle.

Dan had phoned ahead after he heard that Claire and the babies were ready to leave the hospital, and a welcoming party was waiting for them including Jessie, who had arrived home from school, and her assistant, who'd been there in time to greet her. After a few minutes of oohing and aahing by everybody, Dan shooed them all away.

Claire, feeling suddenly weak from the trip home and all the excitement, settled into the big recliner in the family room to nurse Isabella while Dan sat down with Isaac. Jessie's assistant parked Jessie in her chair close by and then busied herself emptying the bags brought home from the hospital and making a cup of tea for Claire at her request. The newly enlarged family was left alone to have a few private minutes together.

After five minutes, Dan gently took Isabella from Claire and handed Isaac to her for his turn at the breast. He patted Isabella awkwardly on the back as he had seen Claire do and was soon rewarded with a big burp. Then he held her gently, rocking her back and forth against his chest while Claire dealt with Isaac who seemed to take longer to nurse than Isabella and with more interruptions.

Dan had been given two months paid paternity leave by his company and he sat there now with a dazed look on his face. "You're still having trouble taking this all in, Dan," Claire said softly.

"Aren't you?" he responded. "It seems unreal, too much to expect, too good to be true." He could have said more, for both he and Claire had already noticed how responsive the babies were, but he was sensitive to Jessie sitting there beside them with a quizzical look on her face. He got up and placed Isabella in her lap, still holding onto her to make sure she didn't fall. Dan took Jessie's right hand and placed it gently against Isabella's face and Jessie laughed.

Just then Marie, Jessie's assistant, returned to the room with Claire's tea and Claire motioned to her to get the phone out of Claire's purse and take a picture. It was never easy to get a picture of Jessie with her beautiful but very fleeting smile but somehow Marie managed this. At the last second, Dan backed away, trusting that Jessie could hang onto Isabella safely long enough for the picture to be taken. Marie then took a second picture of Claire with Isaac and with Dan standing beside them. The two pictures, enlarged and beautifully framed, sat in a place of honor in their living room for all the years to come, reminding both Dan and Claire of that special moment when they began their new life as a family of five.

Chapter 26: The New Normal

The next two weeks passed in a sleep deprived daze as Claire and Dan struggled to develop a workable routine for meeting the new babies' needs. Regular after school help was arranged for Jessie but she was fascinated by the twins and wanted to spend most of her time while at home with them. Marie saw this and in the time not devoted to meeting Jessie's particular needs she gradually took over a good number of other household tasks plus some meal preparation, freeing Dan and Claire to focus on the twins and Jessie.

Isabella was soon able to sleep three to four hours a night without waking, but Isaac was having more difficulty, waking and crying much more frequently. Claire worried about this and there were frequent phone calls to the clinic as a result. One day a week after their return home, Claire mustered the energy to take the babies back to the pediatrician for a check-up. Dr. Newton checked them over and found that Isaac was not gaining as well as Isabella. He did discover that Isaac had a small tongue-tie that he clipped in the hope that this would allow him to suck more efficiently. He sent them off after instructing Claire to begin supplementing Isaac with bottle feedings of formula so that it would be easier for him to suck in more milk, and to return in a week so his weight could be checked again.

The next week passed slowly with Claire fully preoccupied in making sure that Isaac took in enough milk, much easier with bottle than breast since that way she could actually measure his intake. But she still tried to breast feed him as often as she could since she knew how important that was for developing his immune system. Whatever spare time was left over from meeting the babies' immediate needs and carrying out the other necessary household chores and meal preparation was spent with Jessie who, in her own way, was beginning to show signs of resentment over her mother's divided attention.

In the wee hours of the night after waking to feed and change one baby or the other, Claire snuck in a few minutes searching the internet for anything she could find on low birth weight, or on differential nutritional availability and growth restriction in the womb in the case of twins. As well, she perused various studies suggesting overall differences in intelligence level between twins and singletons, particularly in the case of the lower birth weight twin. This did not leave her much time for mulling over Caroline's unsolved murder.

After the first six weeks passed, a more or less regular routine was in place in the Marchyshyn houschold. Both babics wcrc slccping up to four hours a night now but Isaac was almost completely on formula with only an occasional turn at the breast. Isabella, always hungry, also had the occasional bottle but managed mostly with breast milk.

Isaac had been gaining weight and was now only slightly behind Isabella. He was also more alert than he had been initially and beginning to reach out for objects, something Isabella had been doing for a while. Claire still worried about the difference between them but visitors were quick to comment on how lively and curious they both were and the pediatrician was pleased with Isaac's progress. Hence, Claire's previously obsessive focus on her newborn twins was beginning to weaken and she was growing restless.

One day Claire phoned Michael only to discover that no further progress had been made on finding Caroline's murderer and that they were about ready to close the file. This infuriated Claire for she knew in her heart that she'd put Sergeant Crombie on the right track and they had only stalled because of lack of follow through. *I guess I'll have to do it myself, as usual,* she muttered, startling Annie, the new assistant they had hired for three mornings a week to help out with housework and baby care.

That night Claire complained to Dan about feeling stir crazy and managed to look so sad and bedraggled that he himself suggested she dress up and go out, maybe with Tia, for an evening's change. He would stay home since neither of them wanted to leave the twins solely in charge of somebody else at that point.

The next morning, a Saturday, Claire phoned Tia and managed to slip out of the house and meet her for coffee at a near-by Starbucks since it was Tia's day off and Dan was home. Jessie's assistant was there as well and between the two of them, they assured Claire that they could care for the three Marchyshyn children for a couple of hours.

Claire updated Tia on the case and shared her frustrations and suspicions with regard to Caroline's murderer. "The only way we'll ever get him is to set a trap for him and get him to confess," Claire proclaimed. "And," she added, "we can't expect any help from Michael given Stan's complaint to Donald about harassment."

"Are you going to ask Sylvia for help?" Tia asked.

"No! And don't you say anything to her either!"

"Look, Claire, I know you don't like her and you resent the way she worked herself into McCoy's good graces, but can't you get over that? We may need her help!"

"Okay," Claire said. "I admit that I've been feeling a bit jealous and resentful. But I really think that in the interests of finding Caroline's murderer I'd be big enough to rise above that. There's more to it, though. My gut is telling me not to trust her. She could have told us more about Caroline's life earlier on and we would've been able to proceed a lot more rapidly. And I don't entirely buy her high-minded morality motive for holding back at the time. There's something more to it than that. I can just feel it—and I've learned to trust my *feelings!*"

Tia looked at Claire fondly and said, "Okay—and I've learned to trust them too. We'll play it your way."

"Well, I don't actually have a 'way' yet. I've got to do some more thinking, but I just had to see you today so I could bring you up to speed and get you on my side to help me. Thanks, Tia," Claire said gratefully. "Thanks for understanding and for trusting me." Tia and Claire spent a few minutes more engaging in baby talk and then it was time for Claire to get back to her domestic responsibilities and for Tia to deal with all the household issues she couldn't address during the rest of the week.

Chapter 27: Claire's Night Out

Tia and Claire had agreed that next Friday night would be the best time to carry out the next part of the plan since Tia didn't have to work on Saturdays. Dan suggested that she meet Tia for dinner at a nice restaurant.

"No," Claire replied. "I don't want to leave the babies that early. I'll just meet up with her later after they're both asleep."

"But where will you go, a movie?"

"No. I just want to visit. We'll just go to some quiet place and have a couple of drinks." Dan looked at her suspiciously but said nothing. It was definitely not like Claire to pass up the chance for a meal out.

At nine that evening, the two friends, Tia and Claire met at the bar Ronald was in the habit of frequenting. Tia regarded it doubtfully. "It looks like a bit of a dive. Are you sure this is a good idea, Claire?"

"No, I'm not sure. But it's the only lead I have."

Tia shrugged and they entered the bar and found their way to a booth in the back corner. They both ordered wine and sipped away on their drinks cautiously. "Beer would last longer but then I'd have to use the washroom every ten minutes," was Claire's comment. She opened her mouth to add something but Tia held up her hand warningly.

"There's a man and woman just settling into the booth ahead of us on the other side," she said.

Claire pulled the picture of Ronald out of her purse and handed it to Tia. "Is it him?" she hissed.

"Yes, and the woman he's with is small and dark haired but she's way back in the corner of the booth and I can't see anything else."

Tia and Claire sat back in silence then and when the waiter came by to check on them, they ordered water and a plate of nachos. The latter was Claire's idea. As she explained to Tia, "We need to soak up the alcohol so we can stay alert!"

Tia nodded and smiled but she knew that wasn't Claire's only motive. She knew Claire too well.

At first there was little evidence of conversation from the booth where Ronald and the girl were seated. They heard a drink order being given but couldn't quite make out what it was. After it arrived—what appeared to be a gin and tonic and a tall draft beer—they did begin to hear some snatches of conversation and gradually the voices rose higher.

"Why have you been so busy lately? I hardly ever get to see you!" Ronald complained.

The woman replied in a soft, soothing voice but neither Claire nor Tia could make out her words. The server arrived then with their nachos. "Here you are, ladies. Enjoy!" he said in a loud enough voice that it caused the heads in the other booth to turn and made Claire wince. The two women hunched back in the corner and bent over their nachos without risking any further conversation. They noticed that the conversation in the other booth appeared to have ceased as well.

Another ten minutes passed and Claire realized there was no way around it. She needed to use the washroom and the only way to reach it was by passing in front of the other booth. She kept her head well turned away but on the way back she heard a slight gasp as she passed. When Claire settled back into her seat, she and Tia heard voices again from the other booth and this time they were loud enough to hear because Ronald was clearly irritated.

"We just got here and I haven't seen you in ages. Why do you want to leave?"

"I just do. That's all."

"Come back to the house with me then. I have your gin and tonic there and Dad's out of town so we'll have the place to ourselves."

"Oh, I don't know," was the reply in what sounded like a nervous voice.

"You can't just dump me like this on a Friday night! What's the matter? Is there somebody else?"

"No, No! It's just ... I think I'm getting a headache."

"There's always *something* wrong with you. What's the use of doing all those workouts all the time if you're just going to make yourself sick with them?"

"That's not it!" came the terse response. There was silence for a few minutes then but finally Tia and Claire heard the woman say, "Okay, I'll come over for a little while but I still want an early night. I'll bring my car and meet you there."

"No, I'll drive you and I'll bring you back later to pick up your car. It takes yours forever to warm up."

Tia and Claire didn't hear the response because they were busy putting on their own coats. Claire threw some money on the table, looked regretfully at the half eaten plate of nachos and pushed herself out of her seat. Tia followed and they exited the restaurant and headed toward Tia's car that was parked down the block.

Claire realized with a sudden thrill that they were both back in their old groove. They didn't even have to voice their intentions. Both knew that they'd be following Ronald and the girl!

Chapter 28: A Risky Move

As Tia drove, Claire pulled up the Edmonton directory on her phone and checked for Stan Polansky's address, writing it down on the back of the octagonal-shaped cardboard coaster she'd picked up in the bar. Then she checked to make sure she had the home number McCoy had given her on her phone and placed it on speed dial. She grabbed Tia's phone and repeated the process. Tia grinned, feeling the same simultaneous thrill and fear of adventure as Claire.

"Let's turn at the next corner and take a different route," Claire suggested. "That way there's less chance of them realizing they're being followed." Tia agreed and when they arrived at the Polansky house ten minutes later, they saw the car Ronald had been driving parked on the street in front. Tia parked a few spots back from it and they quietly got out of the car.

The Polansky house was of an older vintage, tall and narrow and set on a narrow lot with no trees or fence around it. Only a few shrubs scattered here and there broke the severe lines of the brown brick that encased it, offering little cover for anyone trying to get close without being noticed.

'Now what?" Tia asked.

"Let's circle around to the back," Claire suggested. It's dark there so we'll have less likelihood of being seen."

Cautiously, Tia and Claire crept up to the back door and listened but they could hear nothing. There was a faint light coming from inside and another light upstairs. "Do you think they're up there?" Tia hissed.

"I don't know," Claire replied nervously, her hand firmly cradling the phone that was in her pocket.

They waited a couple of minutes more and then Claire made a decision. Carefully, she turned the handle of the back door and discovered that it was unlocked. She cracked it open slightly and peered inside. It was a back entrance that led up a couple of steps to another door, possibly a kitchen. Tia pushed Claire to one side so she could mount the steps. "Stay out here and be ready to call McCoy if you have to," she whispered.

Tia climbed the stairs lightly and listened at the inner door but there was still no sound. After several minutes, she turned the handle gently and peered inside. It *was* a kitchen and it had been occupied recently. A half empty gin bottle and almost new bottle of tonic water were out on the counter. Tia returned to Claire to report what she'd found and discuss what to do next.

"We have to find out who the girl is. We need to go in there," Claire asserted.

"It could be dangerous," Tia countered. "From what I overheard, he didn't sound that stable to me!"

"Then the girl could be in danger as well. The problem is we just don't know and we can't find out by standing out here. Did you happen to see any kind of closet in the kitchen where we could hide?"

"Yes, but for all we know it's full of stuff and we won't fit and will probably make a lot of noise trying."

Claire was very frustrated. They were so close and she just knew she was right. She also knew she was unlikely to have another chance to finally put this mystery behind her. "I'm going in," she told Tia. "Keep your phone ready. I'll text if it's okay—and call McCoy if anything goes wrong. Here's the address." She handed Tia the coaster, pulled a mini-flashlight out of her purse and crept up the steps. After listening a minute, she quietly opened the inner door, spied the closet directly to the right of the door and crept over to it.

The pantry door creaked ever so slightly when she opened it and Claire froze. When there was no response, she flashed her light inside and saw that it was largely empty. She crept inside, closed the door and texted Tia, warning her about the creak. A few minutes later, Tia was by her side, having managed somehow to open the door less noisily than had been the case for Claire. They both sat down on the floor and stared at each other, wondering what to do next. But they didn't have long to wait.

"Come on, let's have another drink," Ron urged, his footsteps sounding on the kitchen floor.

"I really think I should get going," came the reply from the girl.

"What *is* it with you? It's Saturday tomorrow. Why can't you just stay the night? I told you, Dad won't be home until tomorrow evening."

"No, I think I better go. I can call a cab. I really don't mind."

"*Look!* This is just stupid. Are we in a relationship or not—or is there something you're not telling me?"

"No, no... it's just...."

"There *is* something! You're just like her—stringing me along."

"Who? What are you talking about?"

"She was fine hanging out with me when there was nobody else better around. She didn't mind me spending money on her, taking her places. Always wanting more...urging me to get more...steal even. And she stole from me, too. I know she did. We'd have a hot necking session and the next day there would be money missing from my wallet."

"*I* don't steal!" the woman cried. But Ronald went on as if he'd never heard her. "Silly bitch! Who did she think she was, anyway?"

"*Who* stole from you? You're not making any sense?"

"*You* know who—Caroline!" Tia and Claire heard a gasp.

Claire stopped listening and pushed the 'five' button on her phone to speed dial McCoy. His phone rang several times and Claire began to worry. *What if? What if he's not there? I never thought about that. What can we do then?* she asked herself. But just then the phone was picked up. "Who's this?" McCoy asked in a rough voice.

Claire thought rapidly. They were only a few feet away from the two in the other room. She could easily be overheard. "It's Claire," she whispered. "Hang up; I'll text." She clicked out of the call and then switched to text message. Rapidly she wrote, "We are in Stan Polansky's house. His son, Ron, is the murderer. Come quick. Something bad is about to happen." Tia handed Claire the coaster with the address on it and Claire typed it in and hung the phone up.

Tia still had her ear to the door and now she hissed at Claire. "It's the same Caroline. Listen!"

Ronald was half crying now and his voice was rising higher and higher. "And when I met her again in that gym she was just the same. And she was still so beautiful ... but afterwards she looked so ugly. I couldn't understand that. Maybe the devil inside her came out when ..."

"When what?" the woman asked fearfully.

"She still called me 'Ronnie'" he said, his voice now almost a whisper as if he were remembering something he didn't want to remember. "But just when she wanted something." His voice was louder again. Angry. "And then when I tried to get close to her she'd push me away. And I'd plead with her. She liked that ... She loved to see me crawl." Ron's voice was filled with hurt and anger and he was quiet for a moment, reliving his memories. "Well, no more crawling! I'm not crawling anymore. No more begging from you bitches for me!"

There was a shuffling noise and then the voice of the woman. "I'm sorry you had such a rough time with her. I'm just going to leave now," she said, "and you rest."

"Oh, no, you don't!" Ron's voice was harsh now. "I can't let you leave now. You know too much!"

"I don't know anything! I have no idea what you're talking about!"

"Oh, I think you do. Because you're just the same!" After a pause he went on. "Anyway, it's too late now. You made me so mad that I told you about Caroline. I don't have a choice."

There was silence then and Ronald went on. "It didn't take long, you know. Not long at all. I was surprised. You won't suffer. I'll do it right so you won't suffer. I don't want you to suffer, Sylvia," he said almost lovingly.

Claire and Tia, listening so hard they were practically unable to breathe, looked at each other unbelievingly! "Sylvia! It was Sylvia all along!" Claire hissed.

"You were right about her, Claire! But now's not the time!" It was clear that Ronald was now thoroughly unhinged. There was no more time for waiting.

They looked at each other and Claire frantically flashed the inadequate penlight around the room. Tia grabbed a heavy-bottomed pan hanging on the wall and

Claire chose a large jar of pickles. Then, seconds later, they burst out of the room.

Ron's hands were around Sylvia's neck. "I'm sorry," he said, his eyes solely on her. "I'll make it quick."

Sylvia was struggling and Ron had his legs braced wide apart and was leaning over her squeezing her throat, fully focused on the task at hand. Tia raced at him to bash him over the head with the pot but at the last moment he sensed her and twisted around, still clutching Sylvia's throat. The pot landed on his shoulder instead of his head and Ron threw Sylvia violently against the wall and grabbed Tia's wrist. She screamed in pain and dropped the pot.

Claire came up behind him and tried to hit him with the pickle jar but it bounced off his back harmlessly and rolled away into a corner.

Ron faced them furiously. "You women! Spies! Miserable bitches!" He grabbed Claire and threw her down, slamming her head against a coffee table. She didn't move. Then he lunged at Tia, his face a mask of rage. But at that moment, Don McCoy burst through the door with his gun raised.

Chapter 29: McCoy Saves the Day

Inspector McCoy stood with his legs spread for stability and his gun pointed firmly at the center of Ronald Polansky's chest. "Stop!" he bellowed. "Stop or I'll shoot!"

Ronald froze in place and seconds later two officers arrived and took charge of him while the inspector took in the scene. Sylvia was still on the floor leaning weakly against a wall and rubbing her throat. Tia had sunk shakily into a chair but was otherwise all right. But Claire still lay crumpled against the coffee table, the front of her jacket soaked.

"Call an ambulance!" McCoy demanded an officer in a shaky voice. "She's been shot!" he said, kneeling beside her.

Tia glanced at Claire and quickly realized what had happened. She rose and placed a hand on McCoy's shoulder and said softly, "It's okay, Don. It's just the milk. It's time to feed the babies!"

"Oh!" he said, embarrassed.

His partner arrived then. The inspector had called him from the car during his frantic drive over, and Sergeant Crombie quickly took in the scene. Then he stripped off his jacket and wrapped it around Claire who was awake now and shivering violently. He felt the bump on her head and asked if he should call for an ambulance. But the vigorous way Claire shook her head in response made it clear that she wasn't in much pain and that she definitely was not ready to leave this scene behind her!

McCoy glanced at Claire with a clear look of relief on his face but then focused on the job at hand. He read Ronald Polansky his rights and instructed the two officers to take him to the station and book him on 'attempted murder'. "Nobody is to talk to him until I get there," he snarled. He then turned his attention to Sylvia.

"Are you all right?" he asked her. "Do you want to be checked out at the hospital?"

"I don't think I need to go," she croaked. "If my throat is still this bad I'll go in the morning." McCoy solicitously helped her into a chair and Crombie motioned to Claire and Tia to take two of the other chairs arranged around the table. Donald McCoy sat down in the remaining one and Sergeant Crombie pulled in a small arm chair from the adjoining room and settled himself in it. He got out his minicomputer and prepared to take notes but the inspector asked him to bring in the recorder he always kept in his car.

Finally they were settled and the interview with Sylvia began, with Tia and Claire sitting back silently. 'How long have you known Ronald Polansky?" Donald McCoy asked Sylvia, once he had the preliminaries on file.

"I met him a few months ago." Sylvia coughed and rubbed her throat and Sergeant Crombie got up to get her a glass of water. After another minute, she went on. "At the Spa. He was helping his father there and I came in one morning early before they left." She stopped to cough again and they waited patiently for her to continue. "They were working at night so as not to disturb the clients."

"What were you doing here at his house?"

'We were in a kind of relationship," Sylvia coughed again and then glanced sheepishly at Claire and Tia.

"For how long?" McCoy asked curtly, his tone indicating that he was now beginning to appreciate what Claire had been saying about Sylvia's tendency to prevaricate.

"Oh, maybe two or three months," Sylvia said vaguely. "It wasn't really going anywhere as far as I could see but *he* seemed to feel differently."

"Why didn't you just break it off then?"

"Well, it was a bit awkward." She coughed again.

"In what sense?"

We-l-l-l," Sylvia replied, squirming slightly in her chair, "it got complicated."

"How?"

"He was always doing things for me and I guess I figured I owed him something." Sylvia had a violent coughing spell then and drank the rest of the water. Sergeant Crombie got up to refill it.

"What kind of things?" Don McCoy asked.

"A couple of weeks ago he took me to Reno and..."

Claire couldn't remain silent any longer. She turned to Sylvia and spoke with uncharacteristic restraint, as if she didn't trust herself to acknowledge what she was feeling. "You knew he was a possible suspect in Caroline's murder. Yet you did everything possible to get me off his track. Why?"

"Because I thought you were wrong. Because I liked him and thought you weren't giving him a fair shake." Sylvia lowered her head then and her next words were practically inaudible. "Because you were so sure you had the answer and it just annoyed me." Sylvia coughed again and looked very exhausted.

"Well, you paid a price for that, didn't you? And it could have been a much higher price!" Claire pointed out, turning away in disgust.

McCoy spoke into the tape recorder then. "Interview ending at 12:05 a.m.," he said after glancing at his watch. He looked suddenly old and tired. Turning to Sylvia, he said, "We'll continue this interview tomorrow after you've had a chance to rest and your throat has recovered some. If you like, I can assign a policewoman to stay with you tonight."

Sylvia shook her head, looking miserable.

Don McCoy addressed his sergeant then. "Would you please take Tia and Sylvia back to their cars and then take Claire home. Talk to Dan—about all of it," he said, nodding at Claire. Michael Crombie gave him an understanding look and nodded his head.

When Sergeant Crombie and Claire reached her home, he guided her to the door and rang the bell. Dan answered and looked from one to the other with surprise. "Go to bed, Claire," Sergeant Crombie instructed her. "I'll talk to Dan." And he did just that.

Chapter 30: Wrapping It All Up

Claire was still awake when Dan crawled into bed beside her half an hour later and she braced herself for the tongue-lashing she was sure would follow. But he just put his arms around her and held her close for a few minutes without saying anything. Finally he spoke. "I'm just glad you're safe. Michael told me everything. He even mentioned something about a possible bank heist. But surely that part wasn't true, was it?"

"It's not easy to solve these murders," Claire replied soberly. "Sometimes you just have to think outside the box."

Dan chuckled at that. "Go to sleep and enjoy it while you can, Claire. The munchkins should be up in an hour!" But the twins must have somehow realized what a 'hard day's night' it had been, for they both slept peacefully for another three hours!

The next day, Claire did her own explaining and Dan began to realize the double track her mind had been working along since Caroline's murder eight months earlier. "I've been feeling like you were only partly here for a long time. I couldn't understand why you weren't more invested in the twins. Sometimes it seemed like you didn't care, like you didn't really love them."

"I know. I was preoccupied. I couldn't give myself to them completely because I was always being haunted by this giant piece of unfinished business. But it's over now. Things are going to be different from here on in."

"I hope so," Dan responded, hugging her. "Now if only nobody else will get murdered under your nose for a while so you don't have to feel responsible for solving it!"

Claire hugged him back. "I just want to be here... really getting to know them, enjoying this time, all the things they can do. I don't want to miss anything!"

Dan nodded his head happily.

It was three days later on a Saturday afternoon that they had the big get-together. Donald McCoy and Sergeant Crombie were there; Amanda came with Matthew; and Tia, Jimmy, Mario and Marion arrived and all settled on the sofa together. Aunt Gus and her husband, John, were away on another cruise but Hazel and Roscoe were able to join them since Hazel was working that Saturday at the co-op.

Roscoe hugged Claire, happy to see her—but spent most of the time playing with the twins or holding one or the other of them. Claire regarded these tender interactions with misty eyes and a plan suddenly popped into her head. Tia would be the twins' Godmother, of course, but she would ask Roscoe to be their Godfather. *I don't like Jimmy that much, anyway, but, of course, it could be a little awkward to exclude him,* she ruminated to herself.

As a result of this rumination, Claire missed the first part of the case summary that Donald McCoy was providing but picked it up just as she heard him say "... there were early signs of mental instability. Ronald used a lot of marijuana as a teenager and had a couple of psychotic breaks for which he was hospitalized. He's supposed to be on medication but doesn't always take it. According to his father, he functions more or less okay at times but then something sets him off and he starts to decompensate."

"What does 'decompensate' mean?" Hazel asked. She was always eager to learn something new.

"According to the psych types," McCoy replied, a slight sneer in his voice, it just means he can't keep his sh…"

Michael Crombie interrupted at this point, anticipating that McCoy was about to say something inappropriate. "From what I understand," he said smoothly, "we all have our defenses in this world that keep us going and allow us to function normally. But under extreme stress, and especially if a person is predisposed in some way, these defenses can break down and then we don't function so well. We behave in ways we don't normally behave. That apparently is what happens to Ronald. He has this weakness. His mother knew it and she has protected him all these years and made excuses for him. He's never been able to keep a job but he supposedly has been quite stable lately and she thought he'd be okay living with his father."

"But why did Caroline even get involved with somebody like that back in high school?" Tia asked. "She was apparently so popular!"

"I've talked to some of the teachers there," Michael replied. "She was popular with the guys but not the girls. She was very attractive but just not on the same wavelength as other girls her age. She didn't fit in with them but the guys liked her—for a reason." He stopped talking at that point and left them to draw their own conclusions.

"But I still don't understand why Ronald killed her?" Claire interjected.

"When he got home from the bar that night he apparently took some uppers and got all jazzed up and decided to work out. For months he'd been using his father's key to access the gym early in the morning before anyone else was there, and had begun to regard it as his own territory. When Ronald saw Caroline lying on the table that he always used and lifting his favorite dumbbell, with what he described as a smug look on her face, he just lost it."

McCoy interrupted at that point and took the story forward. "Ronald had met Caroline at the gym one early morning a couple of months previously when he had been working with his father. She'd been nice to him at first and they'd gone out a few times. He had some money at the time and what he had he spent on her: restaurants, flowers, and other things she fancied. But when the money ran out she seemed to lose interest in him, started pushing him away. So he was already angry with Caroline when he came into the gym that morning and seeing her like that just pushed him over the edge."

"Ugh," was all Claire could say. "What's going to happen to him now?"

"He's in a forensic psych ward and that's probably where he'll stay. It's not clear at this point whether or not he's fit to stand trial. He had another breakdown after his confrontation with you two the other night," and he glared at Claire when he said this.

"I don't know what you're looking at me like that for," she said boldly. "If Tia and I hadn't been there Sylvia would have become his second murder victim!"

"Yes, and if I hadn't been home to answer your call, you and Tia would have become numbers three and four. I almost went downstairs for a swim that evening––we have a pool in my apartment. I wouldn't have had my phone with me if I'd done that!"

"He didn't have a gun," Claire replied. "Between the three of us I'm sure we would've been able to subdue him eventually. He couldn't have taken us all down with his bare hands!"

"Well, fortunately we never had to find out," was all McCoy would say.

"And that's it?" Claire replied. "No 'Thank you for finding the murderer, Claire'? 'Thank you, Claire and Tia, for saving Sylvia's life.' Just 'You didn't play by the rules so you're a bad girl and I had to swoop in to save the day,'—and, of course, take all the credit!"

There was a collective gasp in the room for this time Claire had surely gone too far and only Tia understood the full implications behind it. She got up now and moved over to stand beside Claire and put her arm around her.

Michael jumped in then to try to get them past the awkward situation that had been created by both parties. "You're right, Claire. We probably wouldn't have solved Caroline's murder without your help and it is quite likely that if you and Tia hadn't followed Ronald home that night Sylvia would have died. But Donald is only saying that it came at too high a cost. You both placed yourselves in a very risky situation and even, as you say, if the three of you could have fought him off you still could have been very seriously injured. What Donald has simply been saying is that you take chances you should not take for your own sake!"

"Well, it's done now," said Claire. She turned to McCoy and added, "And the next murder you're going to have to solve on your own because, as you see, I'm going to be quite busy."

Donald McCoy looked grim but said nothing.

"*I* hep!" Roscoe said, looking fondly at the babies.

Tia spoke at that point. "I'm curious to know what's happening to Sylvia. I invited her here today but I haven't heard from her."

Claire turned to Tia at this point looking shocked and angry. "Later," Tia whispered.

"Sylvia is very upset and remorseful over what happened," Michael replied.

"Apparently she's been trying to call you, Claire, but you haven't been answering your phone."

Claire made no response but her face was set in a stubborn cast.

The meeting ended shortly after and everyone left but Tia. She wanted to remain behind for a bit and Claire promised to drive her home later. Tia looked meaningfully at Dan and said, "I need to talk to Claire alone for a little while." Dan looked at her but didn't ask any questions for they both knew what the issue was.

"I'll be okay with the twins and Jessie for a bit," he said, turning to Claire. "Why don't you take Tia into the family room?" Claire nodded and thanked him.

Chapter 31: Epilogue

"What?" Claire asked defensively, once she and Tia were settled into the two comfortable recliners in the family room, each with a cup of tea.

Tia looked at her friend and contemplated how to begin. Finally, she said, "Have you ever looked closely at Sylvia?"

"Of course I have!" Claire said impatiently.

"I mean," Tia went on, "how would you describe her face?"

"I don't know ... just a face."

"You once called her 'weasely'" Tia prompted. "What did you mean by that?"

"Nothing. Oh, maybe I meant she was kind of watchful and crafty."

"On the defensive?" Tia asked.

"Yes...no. *I* don't know. Where is all this going?"

"Would you say she had a pretty face?"

"I don't know. I never thought about that."

"Did you ever wonder why she was well into her thirties and still single?"

"No, I just thought she was busy with her life and not ready to settle down."

"What life? Did she ever talk about her life outside the gym?"

"No, but we weren't exactly buddy-buddy. "I just saw her as..."

"You saw her as useful—somebody who could help you find Caroline's killer ... but you never saw her as somebody you would want for a friend, did you?"

"Why should I? Her personal life was not my problem."

"I agree," Tia said evenly. "But this is what I think you didn't see. "Sylvia is not attractive. Her teeth stick out a bit and her chin is a little retracted. Her face is kind of thin and flat looking and her body is not particularly well formed. She's not fat but she doesn't have an attractive feminine shape either."

"I never noticed and I certainly don't care about that. That's not why I was uninterested in having a closer relationship with her. We just didn't click—too different."

"No-o," Tia said in a measured tone. You didn't 'click' because you were the same in a certain way."

"How? She was timid and conventional and legalistic. That *hardly* describes me!"

"But you both have felt chronically inadequate about your bodies—you for no good reason: you have an attractive face and a good build. Your biggest problem is a few extra pounds that you could lose with a little self-discipline. Sylvia, by contrast, is not at all attractive. She knows it and acts accordingly. When Ronald, on the rebound from the beautiful Caroline, took an interest in her it must have been a real ego boost. It's not surprising that she couldn't allow herself to see him as having anything to do with Caroline's murder."

"Wouldn't she just see herself as second best after Caroline rejected him? How is that an ego boost?"

"But that's just it! I don't think she knew he was seeing Caroline, that he even *knew* Caroline. I don't think either one of them would have mentioned it to her. But that's something I'm going to ask Michael to check on. He said they'd be visiting Ronald next week because they had a few further questions for him."

"If what you say is true," Claire responded, thinking rapidly, "that means she was really lying to herself, not to us!"

"How is that?" Tia asked.

"She needed to believe he cared about her, that he saw her as desirable. But then she began to see through him, to see *his* limitations and *his* hang-ups. It reflected back her own negative feelings about herself and then she didn't want him anymore."

"And," Tia added, those negative feelings are probably why she tried so hard to please McCoy and was so pleased when he responded positively! And why she had to tell us about it just to make herself feel better, like she was important, too!"

"Now she's probably feeling extra bad about herself, kicking herself for her bad judgment—and she's probably feeling awful about the way she misled us. I should call her!" Claire replied.

Tia just shook her head. This was so Claire! Now that she wasn't feeling threatened about Sylvia worming her way into McCoy's confidence she could afford to be magnanimous and her naturally generous nature was re-emerging. She opened her mouth to reply but it was already too late.

Claire in her impulsive way had already picked up the phone, flicked back to Sylvia's last call and pushed the redial button. When Sylvia answered, Claire apologized for not getting back to her, using the twins as an excuse for being too busy. "We missed you at the meeting today," Claire went on. "Tia told me she invited you."

"I have been busy packing. I leave tomorrow."

"Leave? Where are you going?"

"I'm moving back to Calgary and will be staying with my family for the time being. Once I get a job there I'll move out on my own. I think I've had enough of Edmonton after all this!"

"Moving! What about your apartment?"

"I was just renting it by the month. I've been considering the possibility of moving for a while. There doesn't seem to be much here for me," Sylvia said with a sad but resigned note in her voice. "By the way," she added, "is Fergus doing okay?"

"Oh, don't worry about him! He's doing fine and getting spoilt. Mavis is particularly attached to him. Every night, one of the assistants puts Fergus on Mavis' lap for a while and places her hand on his back and they just sit there like that. Fergus seems to understand that she can't really pet him because of her lack of hand control and he tolerates just sitting there like that for a few minutes."

"Oh! That's so sweet!" Sylvia said happily, regaining some of her points in Claire's book. "But what about the others?" she went on. "Do they treat him all right and play with him, too?"

"No, they don't really play with him," Claire said. "Play actually requires a certain amount of imagination and creativity that they don't really have. But Roscoe has taken responsibility for feeding Fergus every night and he gets very upset if anybody else interferes or offers Fergus extra food. He says that he's afraid that Fergus will get fatter and that won't be good for him. I wish Roscoe could apply that same reasoning to himself!"

"Oh," said Sylvia, not catching the irony. "And the third one? There are three of them there, aren't there?"

"Yes. Bill is the third one. He's autistic and he forms strong attachments and has a strong sense of duty. He's the one who regularly cleans Fergus' litter box. Before I left I made sure to arrange with staff to buy only the really good clumping litter that deodorizes. All Bill has to do is to use the litter rake to pull out the lumps and place them in a plastic bag the assistant gives him and then place the bag in the garbage and wash his hands. He has a regular routine worked out and he enjoys it and is very faithful to it!"

"Wow!" Sylvia said admiringly. "I guess that doesn't leave much for the staff to do!"

"No. Their only responsibility with regard to Fergus is to make sure that the litter and cat food are purchased regularly and the litter box is emptied and refilled as needed. And they are gradually training Bill to do that part, too, without spilling it all over the floor!"

"Well, it sounds like Fergus has found his forever home and is a real gift to them."

"He is, Sylvia, so don't worry about him—and good luck in your future life in Calgary!"

They said their good-byes then and Claire hung up the phone. Turning to Tia, she explained the parts of the conversation Tia hadn't overheard or deduced and then said, "It's really all over now, isn't it?"

"Yes," Tia said. "No more mystery. No more loose ends. Back to the old grind."

They looked at each other affectionately and laughed.

THE END

ABOUT THE AUTHOR

 In her private life, Emma and her husband, Joe Pivato, have raised three children— the youngest, Alexis, having multiple challenges. Their efforts to organize the best possible life for her have provided some of the background context for this book and others in the Claire Burke series. The society that the Pivatos have formed to support Alexis in her adult years is described at http://www.homewithinahome.com/Main.html.

Emma's other cozy mysteries in the Claire Burke series are entitled *Blind Sight Solution, The Crooked Knife, Roscoe's Revenge, Jessie Knows, Murder on Highway 2,* and *Deadly Care.*

Made in the USA
Columbia, SC
29 November 2020